Whimsy Michaels and Her Amazing Room

A Novella

By

Lana Lynne

Take Me Away Books, a division of Winged Publications.

ISBN-13: 978-1-946939-52-4
ISBN-10: 1-946939-52-8

For My Granddaughter
Thaylin

Acknowledgements

Whimsy Michaels and Her Amazing Room is a work of fiction. Names, characters, home setting places, and incidents are from the writer's imagination. Other real places mentioned are in association with fictitious events involving the author's characters, and any events, places, or persons associated with these, living or dead, is coincidental.

This contemporary story took me by surprise. My penchant for history leads me to the historical fiction or creative nonfiction romance genre as a rule, but not this time. Characters tap writers on the shoulder. Whimsy hugged my heart and soul. Thank you, Lord Jesus. This story is yours.

Others who share in this hug are the members of my critique group: Vickie Phelps, Linda Burklin, Amber Tinsley, Barbara Arent, and Linda Daniels. Thank you. My gratitude for your honesty and refining input are eternal.

A special thank you to Mary Bohn, you are the definition of a true friend.

The writing journey collapses if the author's support system falters. I am blessed to have an unwavering one. My husband and family never fail. Thank you, Rick Higginbotham. Your love is why I am able to keep writing. Also, big hugs to my father, sister, daughter, son-in-law, and granddaughter.

The wonderful culmination of this came when Cynthia Hickey (Melton) of Forget Me Not Romances accepted my manuscript. Thank you,

Cynthia. Collaborating with you is a joy.

A story isn't real until it reaches a reader's heart. If you are holding this book in your hands, thank you. Enjoy the treasure hunt of *Whimsy Michaels and Her Amazing Room.*

Blessings—

Lana Lynne

CHAPTER 1

The Doorway to Whimsy

Somewhere between whimsical and real, between colored, puzzle-pieced walls—which transformed beyond clockwork design and unmeasured time—sat a little girl. The creak of the rocking chair drew the focus of those who bothered to peek in the room. But they often missed the child. Many stopped after shutting the door to continue down the hall, second-guessing their recollections. Uncertainty bred of what couldn't be and what *must* be. When asked, they all responded the same.

"Yes, we saw Whimsy."

Martha "Whimsy" Michaels to be exact. The whimsical look on her face at birth clinched the name for her father, and her mother said it characterized their daughter more each day. Her brother simply shrugged when people called her odd.

"That's just Whimsy," he'd say with a tolerant smile.

That same yet more knowing smile often appeared on the faces of Whimsy's playmates—if you could call them that. She chose them before they chose her. As a toddler, she selected the special few after a period of studied observation, and took them by the hand, leading them to her chaotic piles of blocks, art supplies, and treasured, excavated contents from her father's desk wastebasket. Those special friends, who waited for her to guide them through her treasures, emerged with unique collages as souvenirs after a period of magical play where time stood still for most. But those who persisted in having their own way lost knowing Whimsy. She didn't want to direct or dictate their play and design. No, not at all. Whimsy cocked her pixie face as she squinted her beryl green eyes in appraisal of her friends' designs. Then she added simple accents or made small adjustments. Wonder and joy showed on the faces of those who caught her insight. Many clapped their hands in glee.

Were these childhood collages brilliant art? No, but something sparkled—an element of the divine within each. No one could explain it.

Her mother said, "Perhaps she's still close enough to heaven to hear angels whisper in her ear."

This could have been true, for as Whimsy grew older and started school, she stopped making the collages for a few years. Her older brother Stephen didn't think much about it until the day she failed to return from church with his parents in her almost eighth year. Sickness kept him home that day.

"Where's Whimsy?"

His parents smiled at him. "She'll be home soon."

She came to see him with her hair still damp. The sparkle present in her younger years could not compare to the new fire in her eyes. He held his breath as she hugged him before dashing to her room next door.

The next day a new wave of playmates started seeking her even as she sought them. Joy and urgency characterized her approach to each day until about two years later. During school hours, Whimsy seemed like a normal child. However, once she came home, she started disappearing into her room. Her parents and brother often checked on her, only to find her rocking in her chair, sometimes smiling, sometimes crying, and sometimes frowning. This characterized her home time except for when her friends visited. Then sounds of music and laughter emanated from under the door after periodic spans of silence. Sometimes, her parents cracked the door to find them making collages or to find they weren't there at all.

"They must have gone outside."

Upon checking and finding both yards empty, they'd return to find them in the room. Her friends often smiled and showed them their artwork before leaving to go home.

Stephen grew tired of this mysterious seclusion by his fifteenth and her twelfth year. He burst into her room to find Whimsy and her friend Emily standing to his left, facing part of the deep red wall framing the door. The vestiges of her once rainbow nursery surrounded them from four sides, each painted a different color. The colored walls remained long after the rainbow mobile and clouds found a new home in her baby trunk in the attic. Only two decorations adorned the walls—one tacked on the blue wall and one on the purple wall. No deep anchor holes marred any of the wall surfaces except the four—compass point positioned—bare nails on this side of the crimson wall. Hairline cracks, imperceptible to most, ran like map lines in the old paint.

"Hey, where have you been? I'm tired of you sneaking around and not getting caught," he said.

Whimsy and Emily exchanged a smile.

"Gotta go, Whimsy," Emily said.

"See ya," Whimsy said before turning to face him.

"I don't know why you play with that cripple anyway," he said, still watching her friend hobble down the hall.

Whimsy sighed and began to put away her collage supplies. He waited.

"No, you don't, but I do, Stephen. And we never left the house. We played "Seek the Treasure" for a bit and finished her collage," she said.

"I thought you finished that last time," Stephen said, lifting an eyebrow.

She gave him a small smile. Her eyes glanced at the red wall. "No, no. Emily's collage took us a few months to finish, but we're finished now."

The odd sensation of missing something coursed through him, filling him with frustration.

"Oh—why?"

"It just did. Some take longer than others do. Some won't be finished until there's no time," Whimsy said. Her eyes glowed as she shut the lid of her art case.

Her last words did not register as Stephen's

mind jumped back. "What's the "Find the Treasure" game? We've never played it. I've never heard of it. Is it like a scavenger hunt?"

A bemused smile appeared on his sister's face. "Yes, in a way."

"How's it different?'

Determination filled Stephen, but Whimsy's penetrating gaze made him squirm after a few seconds. He waited.

"I'll teach you someday," She started to turn away.

Oh, no, she wouldn't get off that easy. Stephen crossed his arms. "I want to learn now."

Their mother appeared in the doorway. "Dinner's ready. Go wash up right now. Your father just got home."

"Yes, ma'am," Whimsy said.

Stephen nodded and waited until their mother headed back down the hall. Whimsy walked around him, and he touched her arm. "Why not now?"

She grinned. "It's dinner time. Besides, you're not ready. I'll teach you when you are." Then she headed for the doorway.

Stephen heard the water running in the hallway bathroom and started to follow, but the presence of the two collages tacked in the corners of opposite walls stopped him. How strange. She had not allowed anything on these walls. An unexpected ripple of excitement or perhaps apprehension went through him. They weren't Whimsy's. One hung on the blue wall and one on the purple wall. He'd never paid much attention to the details of his sister's friends' art until now. The simple one on the purple wall drew him first. A patchwork design of coloring book pages—cut just so, original stick figure sketches, glitter, and buttons adorned the one in a color scheme of gold, crystal, pearl, and purple; unusual in a way he couldn't explain but nothing special. He flinched as his eyes went to the one on the blue wall. The slashes of black, gray, and swirling glass shards, and sharp sticks adorning the foam board backed page disturbed him until he noticed red teardrops falling between each adornment, changing to pure white and blue in a river at the bottom of the page.

His chest constricted until he exhaled the breath he had held since his eyes took in the collage. "Wow—"

"Right?" His father's deep voice made him turn.

"Whose are these?" Stephen asked.

His father stepped up behind him and his gaze returned to the collages.

"Well, the one on the purple wall belonged to little Cindy Martin's."

Stephen reached a hand back to scratch the back of his neck. "You mean the little girl who got baptized the same day as Whimsy?"

His dad nodded. "Yes, but they became friends long before that. Remember them in the preschool days? Her mother is still one of your mother's dearest friends even though they moved."

Stephen swallowed hard. A twinge of guilt gripped him. "You mean after Cindy died? I'd forgotten how close they were. She used to spend the night once a week. No one expected it."

His dad grimaced. "Yes and no. Cindy had a

serious congenital heart condition. It's a miracle she made it past infancy. She and Whimsy started this page in preschool and finished it the day before we took Whimsy to the hospital to see her. Cindy wanted Whimsy to have it."

Stephen's eyes cut to the other one. "And that one?"

"Ask Whimsy." His dad put his hand on his shoulder. "Let's get to the table now."

CHAPTER 2

The Blue Wall

Stephen waited until bedtime to talk to his sister about the powerful collage on the blue wall. He knocked on her door.

"Come in, *Stephen.*"

He frowned as he pushed the cracked door open. "How'd you know?"

Whimsy sat on her bed holding a book, which she laid on her bedside table as he entered.

"Dad mentioned you wanted to ask me about Eric's collage."

A current of shock pulsed within his gut.

"Eric? Like in my best friend Eric?"

She patted the foot of the bed. "Yes, that Eric."

Stephen sank onto the lumpy mattress, the springs squeaking like the protests in his disgruntled heart.

"No . . . no, Eric would have told me. Why would he make a collage with you?" Stephen snorted a half laugh. "Besides, he's never played in your room." He laughed outright.

His sister did not. Instead, she propped up her pillows and scooted back against the headboard, pulling her knees up as she studied him.

He waited.

"You're right. Eric did not come in here until he'd almost finished the collage," Whimsy said.

Stephen crossed his arms. She continued. "Do you remember last year when I came to your baseball games with Mom and Dad?"

He shrugged. "I guess so. But Eric didn't play because—"

"He had a broken arm. But he came to all the games. His parents were going through their divorce, so his mom dropped him off, and he sat with us," Whimsy said.

"So, that's it?"

His sister continued to stare at him with her bright green eyes.

"Come on, Whimsy, spit it out!"

Whimsy's eyes closed at his outburst, but opened, guarded and sad. She sighed.

"He stayed upset for a long time. We made most of his collage at the picnic tables behind the stands at the baseball field," Whimsy said. She yawned and scooted down in her bed, punching the pillow a few times. "Good night."

Stephen stood and moved closer to his friend's posted collage. It chilled him, but brought him hope for some reason. "Whimsy, Dad said—"

His sister's voice sounded muffled against her pillow. "You're not ready. Go to bed."

He hesitated for a moment.

Whimsy reached to turn out the lamp, but stopped and instead propped up on her elbow. Her voiced softened. "Stephen, I'm sorry to irritate you.

I don't mean to. There's so much I want to share with you," she paused for a moment, frowned, and then continued, "when you're ready."

Stephen heaved a deep breath in frustration. "What does that even mean?"

Whimsy sank back on her pillow and smiled, without a hint of teasing. "It means I love you. Good night."

This time she reached over and clicked off the light. Stephen felt his way to the door.

~

Eric, Suzie, Bonnie, Charles, Anne . . . the names and collages associated with the blue wall numbered less than those associated with the red wall but more than those associated with the purple wall and yellow wall. All collages remained in the possession of their respective creators except for the two now in her room. Eric's collage remained the only one on the blue wall at this point. Whimsy remembered the day they started his.

Whimsy noticed Eric as he walked toward the stands with his head down the first afternoon of baseball season. His cast-encased arm hung in a navy sling.

Her mother leaned her head close to Whimsy's. "I hate that Eric can't play. He really needs something to take his mind off of his dad leaving."

Eric lifted his head, scanning the bleachers and smiled when he found them. Her dad motioned him to join them. A big smile erupted on his face and his long legs took the steps by twos. He adjusted his cap with his usable hand and sat beside Whimsy. He leaned forward and turned his head toward them.

"Thanks for letting me sit with you. Our team should take the Falcons today. Stephen's pitching, right?"

Her dad grinned. "Right. I know you miss it."

"Aww, it's not too bad." Eric grinned back. "This cast makes pretty girls talk to me more than before. Right, Whimsy?"

Her mother shot her a look, but Whimsy refused to treat him any different from before. He seemed more like a second brother to her.

Eric grimaced at her silence, but he grinned when she refused to look at him.

"I just got here," he said.

She stood and picked up her tote bag. "Mom, if it's okay, I'd like to go work at one of the picnic tables."

"Don't you want to watch your brother?" Her mother sighed. "Oh, very well, but come back before the last inning. You need to at least see the end."

"Yes, ma'am."

Her mother moved to the other side of her dad so Eric could talk to him.

Whimsy made her way behind the bleachers. Several empty picnic tables remained. Peace filled her. She decided on the middle table, placed her bag on it, and scrambled onto the bench seat. Her bag contained all of her art supplies and a thermos, which she opened and poured water into the cup cap. The shinning paintbrush beckoned her to grab it, so she slid out her blank pages and watercolor palette to comply.

Seven teardrop shaped leaves surrounded a

thorny gray stem like multi-level wings. Her brush moved with graceful and deft precision from the paper to a brisk rinse in the water, followed by a cleansing blot on the thick paper to her right. She bit the edge of the wooden tip of her brush before applying the bristle to the red paint. A cluster of flowers each comprised of two butterfly-splayed petals around a golden pistil appeared. White contrast soon radiated from the center and the petals had a tiny and delicate spike on the east to west sides of each flower. The color of the flowers moved from a red to pinkish hue as she worked.

"Euphorbia splendens or Euphorbia milii. Hmmm—what an interesting choice, Whimsy."

She turned at the sound of Eric's voice by her right shoulder. He hadn't startled her. In a way, she expected him.

Eric took one more glance over her shoulder. He picked up a brittle stick and circled to the opposite side of the table to take a seat, awkwardly inserting his long legs and folding his lithe frame onto the wooden picnic bench. The wind rustled the leaves and the smell of honeysuckle drifted on the air. The breeze blew tendrils from Whimsy's ponytail around her face.

"Most people don't recognize this plant, Eric. I'm impressed."

He shrugged, breaking the small stick into pieces under the weight of his cast. "Science, especially botany, has interested me for a long time. That explains my knowledge of this plant. How about you?"

A flicker of surprise merged with joy inside of

her. “Nothing is a mistake in His hands,” she whispered.

“What?” Eric leaned forward. “I couldn’t understand you.”

She smiled and shook her head. “Church. I learned about this plant at church. The preacher has one growing in a planter in his office.”

A sigh escaped her as she gave her painting one last look and placed it to the side. Then she reached in her bag, pulled out a blue piece of construction paper, and pushed it toward Eric.

He brushed off the debris from the crushed stick off the table with his good hand and chuckled. “Oh, no—Whimsy. I’m not making one of your collages. Besides, I can’t do much with one hand.”

She dug in her bag for her scissors, two deep green pages, and two brown ones. “That’s okay. Just hold that page there. I’ll need it in a minute.”

Eric fingered the blue paper with a suspicious look as she began cutting her pages. The sound of the blades shearing paper with rhythmic timing filled the silence between them.

“How’s the game going?” she asked.

“We’re clobbering them. Stephen is doing a great job pitching. They won’t even miss me this season.”

“But you miss them.” She glanced up as his eyes lost their sparkle and grew serious.

“Yeah, I miss a lot of things.”

She stopped for a moment. “And you can’t do anything about any of them, right?”

His eyes met hers and widened. He gave her one nod. “I guess not. No, not much for me to do these days. To tell you the truth, I'm not doing much more than taking up space at school and home."

Whimsy cut the paper into pointed strips. Once she finished, she started to pick up her paintbrush, but stopped and reached back into her bag. Two small squeeze bottles—one containing red paint and the other black—appeared. She reached in for a plastic plate and placed it in the center of the table. Once she squeezed a silver dollar sized circle of each color on it, she set the bottles aside.

Then she laid down her paintbrush, folded her hands, and looked across the table at her brother's best friend. In reality, he felt like a member of their family. She couldn't remember a time after her fourth birthday that he didn't come to their house at least twice a week.

He's ready.

"I'm sorry about your parents' divorce, Eric."

He flinched. "Thanks."

She slid one of the spiked brown strips from the pile, dipped the tip in the black paint, and laid it aside.

He fingered the pile of strips, rubbing the pieces in absent contemplation. "I don't know about hanging around anywhere anymore."

Alarm coursed through her. Panic tempted her to run get her parents, but a deeper conviction calmed her, in an instant of surrender, as she watched Eric take one of the deep green strips and dip it in the red paint. She kept her seat and licked her lips. The words came.

"Yeah, sometimes we feel that way."

He handed her the strip, and she laid it next to

the other one.

"You get down too, Whimsy?"

"Sure, but I've been on enough treasure hunts to know things go beyond that moment."

"Treasure hunts?" Interest flickered in his eyes.

She scooped the pile of strips in her hands, lifted them above the table, and let them rain down onto the surface; some twirled away and landing on the ground. She smiled and looked at him.

"Yes. They're not easy. You'd have to do a lot of searching and digging."

"How long do they take?"

"That depends how close you are to the real treasure and how quickly you're willing to surrender everything else you find along the way."

He grinned. "Okay, I'll play. What if you find other things you want to keep? And turn back before you find it? What if you think those are enough?"

Her heart pounded and previous experiences brought flashes of hurt, no—more like flashes of grief to her, but certainty kept her talking. "You can, but that only leads you back to where you started with things you can never keep in the end. The real treasure is the only one you can keep forever."

He laughed. "Is this a new video game? Has Stephen played it with you?"

She took another brown strip and dipped it in the black paint. "No, we don't play video games at our house. You should know that. Does Stephen play them at your house?"

"I'm not a snitch, but everyone, I mean, most

people play them. They sure have helped me block out the fighting going on with my parents. It's better for me to fight in the games. Movies help too. I like scary ones and stuff with things worse than what I'm going through. It gets my mind off me."

She took another brown strip and dipped it in the black. "Really? I like movies that have a positive story. Life has too much negative on its own. I don't want to focus on it. But everyone is different."

He shifted and looked around. "Well, we both better get back to the game. It's close to the last inning."

She nodded. "Hey, can you do something for me while I clean up here?"

He strummed the fingers of his right hand on the table edge and rolled his left shoulder, adjusting his arm in the sling. "If I can."

She checked the water colored painting—all dry. She placed it in front of him and handed him the scissors. "You can hold this down with your cast and cut it into strips with your other hand."

"Cut it? You want me to cut up your painting. Why?"

"I'm weaving something out of these other strips and the strips from the painting."

He shook his head. "Whimsy, you make no sense. Then again, you never have. Is there really a treasure game?"

His words didn't hurt her. She knew herself. What people thought didn't change her identity. She smiled. "I know. Humor me. And yes, "Seek the Treasure" is real. Are you brave enough to play?"

"Has Stephen played?"

"No, he's not ready."

"And yet you think I am? I'm a mess."

"Yes, I do. You are a mess right now, and you know it. That's part of the reason you're ready."

He sighed. "Sure. What do I have to do?"

She nodded at the scissors. He started cutting the beautiful painting into strips while she returned all but the strips to her tote. "Okay. First, you need to make a list and drop it by my house. Make a list of all your dark thoughts on one side and the opposite of those on the other side. I'll finish these dipped strips once I have those. Then, I want you to take this blue paper. Look in your room, find the small reminders of key moments—good and bad—in your life, your little mementos, and take pictures of the ones too big to put on this blue paper. You can put them on there in any way you want, but choose each with care. The collage isn't large. It takes time to consider and apply the most impacting items. Don't rush to fill the page. We will meet here for a little bit during every game. "

He adjusted the paper and put down the scissors to flex his fingers a few times. "That's it? Whimsy, that's not a treasure hunt. That's you tricking me into making a collage." He laughed and picked up the scissors.

She let down the invisible shield she held just enough to allow him to see her tear steaked face and earnest heart. "It does seem like it. But, I can say, the collages have never been the point. They are only part of the treasure map and a final memento. It's your choice. Please do this, Eric. You'll have to go on the last part of the hunt alone, but I'll take you to the door."

"Whoa, Whimsy, don't cry." He cut the last of the painting and stood.

She removed two zippered bags from her tote and slid the strips from the painting in one and the green and brown ones in the other. Eric took her tote and waited for her to stand. She pulled her legs from under the table and spun around, pushing off the bench.

Eric bumped her with his shoulder. "Why not? I'll do it. What else do I have going?"

~

During the next game, Whimsy looked up to find Eric ready to join her at the table in the area behind the bleachers. He took his collage home afterward but didn't finish it there. Instead, they met at the same time during all subsequent games that season. Once his cast came off his arm, he started bringing things to add to his collage. He brought a brown paper bag filled with broken glass to their third meeting.

"What's all of this?" Whimsy asked, peering into the bag.

After brushing the heavy blue collage paper with glue, Eric put on thick rubber gloves. He reached into the bag to retrieve varied pieces and shards of multi-colored glass. Unexpected excitement and enthusiasm sparkled in his eyes as he glanced up to answer her.

"These were shot glasses my dad brought me from all his business trips. I now see they weren't special thoughts of me, but his attempt to camouflage a problem as an acceptable souvenir. You see, Whimsy, my dad drinks too much. It started with him having a glass when they had friends over for cookouts or board games. Then he started coming home late after stopping for a drink. The booze is really what's destroyed our family, so I now refuse any reminder of it."

Whimsy didn't respond, but a flicker of joy kindled into a steady flame as she watched him place the pieces into an artistic mosaic of contrasting colors. She noticed the slashes of black lightning bolts painted on one side of his page. He didn't look up and she continued to weave the large coronet of brown and green pointed strips of paper from the two sacks in her bag. She'd started it soon after their first meeting.

Eric had come by to drop off his list of negative thoughts and positive thoughts two weeks after their first meeting. Whimsy had written one thought on each paper strip and dipped the pointed edges of the brown strips in black paint to correspond to the dark ones like anger, revenge, self-loathing, and suicidal thoughts. She dipped the green ones in red for positive thoughts like happiness, triumph, championships, and success. Now, the thick coronet took up her time during the games.

The hours and minutes outside of school during the spring required careful planning as she worked with others besides Eric. Her dear friend Suzy also worked on a canvas of blue, but quite different from Eric's. His showed a dark battle, which could threaten his sanity and life. Suzy suffered from intense headaches and physical pain, which often disabled her ability to function. Both had much to overcome. However, Suzy understood the reality of the ongoing battle and found solace in the composition of inspirational music and paintings along the way, whereas Eric didn't.

Whimsy knew more—anyway, Eric sat with her for about thirty minutes during the third game. He grinned and stood. "Do you mind if I leave this here to dry? I need to go cheer on Stephen. You can throw what's left in the sack away."

"Sure."

After he left, she looked at his work. The weight of the collage might soon overwhelm the heavy construction paper. A 9 x12 piece of foam board should give it better stability. She reached into her bag and found one. Eric could glue his collage to it once his work dried.

The three-month baseball season ended in a middle school championship for their team. A fitting end before Eric and Stephen headed to high school.

Time for their family vacation came just three weeks after school ended. They only had one problem. Whimsy had rescued a dachshund at a special animal adoption event outside the pet store during the last week of school. Her dad agreed to it, but they had no one to care for it while they were gone.

Eric stopped by to pick up Stephen for a movie the first Friday after school ended. The little black dog, which barked and shied away from everyone except Whimsy and her mom, ran up to Eric as he stepped in the door.

"Well, would you look at that," her dad said.

Eric knelt down. "Hey, little fella." He let the dog smell the back of his hand before reaching to scratch one floppy ear.

Whimsy squatted beside him. "His name is Paws. See his tan feet?"

Eric laughed as Paws licked his hand. "Yeah."

Stephen opened the front door. "Come on, Eric. Your mom's honking the horn. We'll be late for the show."

Whimsy touched Eric's arm before he could stand. "Would you ask your mom if you could house sit for us? We don't have anyone to watch him while we're on vacation."

He stood, shifting his weight. "I don't know, Whimsy."

Stephen glared at her. "That's a stupid idea. Why would Eric want to watch your dog? Come on."

Eric shrugged and mouthed, "Maybe" at her.

Stephen walked out the door.

"I'll call your mother, Eric," her mom said.

He nodded and dashed after Stephen.

Eric and his mother lived down the street. That's the only reason his mother agreed. Otherwise, they might have taken Paws to their house, but Eric said his German shepherd did not like other dogs. The one glitch turned out to be Stephen.

He exploded over dinner. "Why can't one of your friends do it, Whimsy?"

Their father looked at him with a raised eyebrow. "Really, son? Whimsy's friends are younger. Your friends are starting High school and Eric lives down the street. He doesn't have to stay here all day. Paws is by himself when we are gone for work and school. He just needs someone to let him out in the mornings, at lunch, and to be here at night. Did you ever think this might be good for Eric and his mother? It's been a rough spring. She doesn't get a vacation from her new job right now. Eric might like a little time out of the house, and it might also give his mother a respite."

Stephen looked down at his plate. "Well, I told Eric he can't sleep in my room."

"Stephen James Michaels, I can't believe you!" his mother said. "Why ever not?"

"Have you ever seen his room? It's a mess. I'm talking a wreck. I don't want mine like that."

His dad laughed. "You're one of the few teenage boys whose room isn't a mess."

Stephen shrugged. "I don't care. I mean Eric *is* my best friend, but his room is ridiculous."

Whimsy cleared her throat. "Have you been in his room lately?"

Stephen took a bite of mashed potatoes and swallowed before he answered her. "No. Come to think of it, I haven't been to his house since the second week of baseball season."

"He did have a broken arm."

Stephen snorted. "No, it stays messy. I think his mother's given up on cleaning it."

"He can sleep in my room," Whimsy said.

Her brother laughed. "You don't let anyone stay in your room."

Her mother's next words pleased her. "That's

not true, Stephen. You don't know your sister very well."

Stephen looked at her for a long moment before ducking his head to finish his food.

After dinner, he stopped her while they cleared the table. "I guess if Eric doesn't mind, he can house sit and watch Paws. But he won't want to stay in your room."

Eric agreed to all the conditions and their family planned to leave after lunch on that Friday. Whimsy climbed in the car last but undid her seat belt almost in tandem with latching it.

"Wait! Stop, Dad. I forgot something."

Her dad hit the brake and shifted into park. "Hurry, Whimsy. We want to get to the hotel before dark. Tomorrow morning will come early, so we can make the rest of the drive to the campground."

"Yes, sir."

She found Eric in the backyard playing with Paws when she dashed through the side gate. Paws bounded over to her, wagging his tail. She scooped him up and laughed at his wet tongue on her face. "Stop, Paws."

She put him down and he ran for his ball.

"What is it, Whimsy?"

"I forgot to tell you, I left something for you by the blue wall in my room and a note by my lamp. Did you bring your collage?"

He took the ball from Paw's mouth, tossed it, and glanced back at her. "Yeah, I did. Hey, when do we get to start on the treasure hunt?"

A broad smile appeared on her face.

He scratched his head and then shook his finger

at her. "See, I knew it. It's all been a ploy to get me to finish a collage."

She wrinkled her nose at him. "Has it?"

"Whimsy!"

She laughed, gave Paws a pat, threw the ball, and dashed for the gate. From the other side, she called, "You'll find it."

~

Eric shook his head. What a funny girl, yet he had to admit he'd changed in the last few weeks. Working on the collage had released a bunch of his feelings, but this unique treasure hunt baffled him.

He felt the ball drop on his foot and looked down into two of the sweetest brown eyes. "Okay, boy, just a few more throws and we'll go get your supper."

After he fed Paws, he pulled the foil off the lasagna Whimsy's mother had made for him. He could microwave it for a few meals and his mother had sent snacks and promised to bring some more things by during the week, plus check on him in person at least once every day.

After he ate, Eric turned on the television but couldn't find anything of interest. He missed his video games but realized he didn't play them as much anymore. His phone dinged, and he smiled at the text from Stephen: *Have you messed up my room yet?*

He responded: *Haven't even opened the door. Where are you?*

Stephen: *Almost to the hotel. We're going to sleep early tonight so we can leave first thing in the morning.*

Eric: *How long will it take you?*

Stephen: *Ten hours tomorrow. We want to reach the campground with plenty of light left to set up our tents.*

Eric: *Sounds fun.*

Stephen sent a crazy emoji face.

Eric laughed and sent a thumbs-up.

He tossed his phone on the table by the couch. The quietness of the house left him uneasy. His backpack sat by the front door. He retrieved it and unzipped the side pocket where he'd packed his toothbrush and extra rubber bands for his braces. The table vibrated as his phoned signaled a call. He picked it up and pressed the screen to answer.

"Hi, Mom."

"How are things going?"

"Fine."

"Do you need anything?"

"No."

"Well, just call me if you do. I'm home now. I'll bring your breakfast."

"Mom, I'm fine."

"Lock up. Call me before you go to sleep."

"Mom, stop. I think I'm going to bed early. Whimsy says Paws might get me up in the night."

"Okay. I love you."

"Good night, Mom."

He shook his head when he discovered the pajamas in his backpack. His mother had pinned a note to them: *Use these. You're staying in Whimsy's room.*

Eric laughed and pulled on the pajama pants. He stuffed his jeans and shirt into his pack and headed to the bathroom. After he brushed his teeth and changed his rubber bands, he opened the door of Whimsy's room. It smelled like fresh linens and Whimsy. The collage on the purple wall drew him to the right side of the room upon entering. He wondered who made it. Odd. It looked nothing like his. This one seemed so innocent. The broken tree twigs overlaying the drawn stick figures of a family of four at the top left and the figures of a family of three with an empty space between the last two people at the bottom right saddened him. A sunburst pattern of gold and purple glitter surrounded crystal and pearl adornments in the void space. Carefully cut and placed small pictures from coloring books filled the middle. The glued pictures started after the last twig figure pictured in the first family, in the upper left corner, and trailed, in three patchwork-patterned rows, all the way to the first person in the family figures on the bottom right. Little buttons dotted the edges of the patchwork placed pictures. Were those someone else's treasures? Something stirred within him, but he dismissed it. He glanced at the lamp on the table beside Whimsy's bed. The small white envelope had his name on it. He reached for it and sat on the bed. The squeak of the springs made him grimace. How would he sleep on this bed?

He slid his finger under the seal and found a single piece of stationery and an old church bulletin. Whimsy's diminutive handwriting on the neat note sparked his curiosity:

Eric,

Where are your treasures? You've found so

many! Yes, you have. Look at your collage. What have you already let go of and what remains? Remember, behind each thing you release, is a treasure. Now you start on the deep digging. I can't assist you anymore. The rest of "Finding the Treasure" is up to you. I've finished my part. It's waiting for you by the blue wall. You will make it through this struggle. It is a battle—stand strong. The victory is already secured, but you must fully walk in the truth of this, and to do so, you must learn to rejoice even while suffering. Even though you've let the dark things steal your focus, those are lies. Find the truth again.

Whimsy

He swallowed hard. Wow, how mature she sounded. Of course, Whimsy always seemed different from other girls her age. His fingers shook as he slid out the church bulletin. Had it only been three years ago? He swiped at the threatening tears. Once his vision cleared and emotions subsided, he looked at the thick brown and green coronet leaned against the right side of the blue wall. Smaller than a wreath but bigger than a flowered head garland, it encircled a smaller paper crown composed of the strips from Whimsy's plant painting. The less scientific name of the plant came to mind—Crown of Thorns—and his heart pounded.

Weariness and a flash of unexpected anger overtook him. He stood and strode over to the wall. Just as he started to grab Whimsy's woven gift and either throw it in the adjacent blue door closet set into the left side of the wall or, better yet, hurl the wreath away, Paws barked. He heaved his breath, clenching and unclenching his fists. The barking continued. He stepped away from the wall.

"Coming, Boy."

The cool night air and the sound of rustling leaves in the oak tree limbs over his head calmed him as he waited for Paws to finish his business. His eyes searched the skies for clear constellations and the North Star. He hadn't prayed since his dad left. No, he didn't just leave; he abandoned them—left no provisions, no address, nothing. If it hadn't been for his grandparents and his mother finding her job, they wouldn't be surviving.

Paws barked and ran to the door.

"Okay, I'm coming."

He got a treat and led Paws to his open kennel in the kitchen. The puppy slept with the door open. Whimsy said he seemed to sleep better in it than on her bed, as long as she left her door cracked for Paws to get her up in the night. Eric planned to do the same.

He grabbed a comic book from his pack and returned to Whimsy's room. He glanced at the purple wall, now on his left, as he lay on the bed and back at the blue wall, now on his right. The bumpy twin mattress squeaked again as he plopped on it, stretched out his legs, and put a hand behind his head. He glanced from the purple wall to the blue wall and twisted to look at the yellow wall behind the headboard. How did Whimsy sleep in here? He bounced a few times. This bed had to be the most uncomfortable one he'd ever found. He tossed and adjusted the flat pillows a few more times but soon gave up on reading.

The interlacing paper strips in the thick coronet caught his eyes again when he reached to turn out the light. It looked more cushioned than the pauper's pillows he had to cradle his head.

An hour later, Eric sat up on the side of the bed. He might have to break his promise to Stephen and change to his room. How did Whimsy sleep on this bed? He stood and turned on the lamp.

"Whoa, too bright."

He squinted and wiped his eyes until they adjusted.

"Wait a minute."

Why hadn't he noticed it before? A sleeping bag sat beside the dresser stool. Eric grabbed it and knelt to unroll it. Perfect. Anything besides that bed. He ignored the flat pillows on her bed and grabbed the fat, woven, double coronet. He squeezed it. Whimy's skill in weaving the thick paper strips into a tight circle gave it stability with only a little crackle. He grinned and reached back for one of the flat pillows. After he turned out the lamp, he knelt, and felt his way to the fluffy down-filled bag by the blue wall. He unzipped it and slid inside. It already felt softer than the mattress.

Eric placed the coronet under the flat pillow and slid his elbow underneath both as he lay on his side in the sleeping bag. One last sigh escaped him before slumber overtook him.

Piercing pain roused him sometime later. He tossed, turning his head side to side, but each movement seemed to make it worse. Images of his dad throwing the bottles his mother had emptied in the sink and his mother's bruised face filled his mind. The memory of him standing between his parents, trying to shield her, taking the blows himself, and breaking his arm merged with flashes of onslaughts from video games as he released his anger. A swirl of feelings warred through him, ranging from rage and betrayal to depression and wanting to end his own life the day of the first baseball game in the spring.

"No, stop—"

The pain intensified. Unknown hands pushed sharp points deeper into his head.

"No, no—"

Voices— jeering, hateful voices—overcame his protests.

"Take him."

The floor, no the wall beside him rumbled, his eyes flew open and blinked away the moisture running in them. Like puzzle-pieced clockwork gears, the blue wall opened to chaos within a scene under a darkening sky. A crowd of people stood ridiculing three men. Some yelled and cried, while others gambled in the dirt. A putrid smell permeated the air.

"Stop! Stop."

His own voice sounded surreal. No! He listened, horrified as he heard himself join the crowd. Fully awake now, he swiped at his eyes—blood, not tears ran into them.

Eric reached his hand to feel the top of his head and winced in pain. He jerked away his pierced fingers and tried to suck out the ache. The woven paper coronet now sat on his head, no longer paper but real thorns.

"Eric."

The kindest voice he'd ever heard called him. He looked up and found the mirror image of how he felt—the Man loomed above him—on a cross. A crown of thorns pushed deep, affixed to the Man's battered and bruised head and face. "Will you share in this suffering with me?"

Eric bowed his head in shame and shuddered. "I accepted you, but I've failed you."

"Eric."

Sobs overtook him at the sound of his name from his—He looked up. "How?"

"Let me take your thorns. Quit trying to take them back."

Eric put his hand to his head again, pain seared through him. "No . . . no . . . can't cause you more pain."

"Eric, you don't understand. Will you let me have your thorns?"

He couldn't stand the pain any longer. "Yes."

The black-tipped brown thorns, dipped in the world's darkness and in the darkest recesses of Eric's mind, unfurled from the coronet on his head. In horror, he watched them shoot like arrows to join the wretched one on the Man's head. The Man shut His eyes and absorbed the pain. Eric reached up and recoiled in pain until contrasting happiness from the red-tipped green thorns still on his head filled him. *Why?* Good things to replace the bad composed these.

"Eric."

He looked up again.

"Will you let me take *these* thorns? All *you*

think is good?"

He fell on his knees. "Yes."

The green thorns representing the opposite to all his pain—including independence from his dad, protecting his mother, and sports championships—left his head and flew upward. As he watched them join the twisted crown on the Lord's head, he realized each one he'd called *good* wasn't—each were traps of pride, vanity, and things the world loved.

The Man looked down, and love radiated from Him. The sky darkened in a curtain of blackness as a barrage of thorns—mixed with nails and swords from all who had been, were, or would be—flew like never-ending quivers of arrows. They appeared as a swarm filled with every sin and darkness, like a plague covered shade. Once pulled down, it blotted out all light.

Eric's eyes and heart felt the enormity of the battle. His mind reeled in remembrance of every scripture he'd ever read when the Man called out for something to drink. They dipped something soft, affixed to a long piece of a Hyssop plant into a pot smelling of vinegar. Hyssop. He also remembered it from the paper he'd written about plants in the Bible for his botany project. Understanding of this plant's significance in verses as part of cleansing and sacrifice culminated. Tears poured down his face.

The Man called out to *His* father and Eric sobbed harder at his last words. He looked down at Eric one more time.

Eric cried out, "Lord!"

No more abandonment.

No more death clothes in any part of his life.

No more—

Eric's shoulders and chest shook and heaved with anguished joy. The Enemy wanted him to tear strips of grave clothes in which to enshroud his life and tear at his mind with thorns of evil and false treasures. The assault against him had been even greater because of his decision at church three years ago.

The repugnant smell formerly permeating the air dissipated, overtaken by a sweet, pleasant aroma he'd never smelled before. Drops of blood and water splattered on him until he lay in a pure crystal blue stream. He felt one last shudder and slept again, dreams of distant gold crowns arranged as letters in the sky spelling "Life" started. He ran with other runners to his right and left toward the horizon.

A wet nose nuzzled him awake. Eric turned his head. Paws whined until Eric sat up, rubbing his face.

"Hey, Boy. Do you need to go out?"

Paws gave one spin and went to the door.

Eric looked at the solid blue wall and found nothing but a neat pile of the strips from Whimsy's painting. He turned the strips over and found scriptures printed there and bowed his head. After a moment, he stood and stumbled to the back door and opened it for Paws.

His dry throat cried for a drink. He reached up into the cabinet and found a plastic cup from the local pizza place. After he filled the cup, he let the stream of water continue to spray on his aching fingers. He gulped down the liquid and refilled it one more time. Over the rim of the cup, the blue numbers on the digital clock on the stove stopped him. No way. Only three hours had passed.

Paws scratched on the door. Eric took one last drink before he put the cup in the sink and let in the sweet puppy.

Paws started for the kennel.

"Hey, you want to bunk with me?"

Paws tilted his head to one side.

"It's okay. Let's try it."

Eric looked at the sleeping bag but found Paws had jumped on the bed.

He smiled. "We've both been rescued."

This time the bumps and squeaks didn't bother him.

CHAPTER 3

The Red Wall

The wind rustled through the pine branches in the tree Stephen gazed at as he lay in the hammock. A gentle sway commenced from the lift of the breeze under the striped material cradling him. He brushed away the hair blowing across his forehead and grinned at the reminder of his barbershop appointment. A quick glance at his watch assured him of another hour before he had to leave. At least he'd finished the mowing early. His dad's job often took him out of town these days so Stephen had charge of the upkeep of the house, as well as the yard. They increased his allowance in lieu of him getting a summer job this year. He felt lucky, unlike Eric, who worked all summer plus after school jobs during the year to help his mother. But you'd never think of it as hard if you talked to his friend. No, Eric didn't complain.

He thought back to the summer three years ago when his friend had house sat for them. Although Eric seemed a bit different afterward, he remained unaware of any thing eventful happening to his friend that week until he'd seen the collage on

Whimsy's wall. He'd thought the change related to Eric's parent's divorce at the time.

After finding the collage on his sister's wall a year later, he'd confronted his friend as they took a few swings in the batting cage at the local miniature golf and game shop.

"Hey, what gives with that collage on my sister's wall?"

Eric adjusted his grip, keeping his eye on the ball popping from the machine and whacked it before turning toward him. He extended the bat. "You're up."

Stephen took it. "Well?"

Eric cleared his throat and spat on the ground before looking at him. "Are you still putting off that decision about church?"

"What?" Irritation gnawed at him. "What's that got to do with anything? You'd joined two years before your parents split."

"True, but I still didn't fully share in it."

Stephen laughed. "Now, you sound like Whimsy."

Eric chuckled. "That's not a bad thing, Stephen. She's all right."

Stephen pushed the button to start the balls. Th-wack! He slammed the ball. "Quit avoiding the question, Eric. We're supposed to be best friends."

He glanced at his grinning friend. Eric's expression became serious. Stephen's focus slipped and he stepped in to the ball too late—strike. He reached to hit the stop button.

"Stephen, you are my best friend, but there are some things I just can't explain to you."

"Why?"

"Because they go beyond understanding," Eric said.

"But you can talk to my little sister about them?"

Eric shook his head. "No, not entirely. Your sister listens and sees from her soul. Don't laugh. She simply helped me change the things I pondered during those tough days. I thought about suicide right after my dad left."

Shock shook Stephen. "Really? Why didn't you talk to me?"

Eric shrugged. "I couldn't. Whimsy gave me the opportunity to find the treasure."

Stephen snorted. "Not you too?"

"Don't dismiss it. I did it while you were on vacation. Do you know Whimsy has never asked me about it since your family drove out of the driveway that day? The day you got home, my mom watched Paws, instead of me, because my dad came by to see me. I'd gone to dinner with him, hoping it meant he planned to come home to us. He didn't, but I remained okay after he left town because of finding the treasure. Anyway, I finished my collage a couple of weeks later and dropped it off with your mom to give to Whimsy."

"If she helped you so much, why didn't you give it to Whimsy in person?"

Eric straightened. "Don't go all big brother protective on me. None of it is about Whimsy."

"It isn't?"

Eric put a hand on his shoulder. "I don't expect you to get it right now."

"Why the—why not?" Anger coursed through him.

Eric sat down on the bench and looked up at him with kindness and candor in his blue eyes.

"You're nowhere near ready."

Not that again—he kept hearing it from Whimsy and now from his best friend, who seemed more like an enemy. His fist made contact with Eric's jaw, knocking him off the bench.

Eric rubbed his jaw but didn't stand, instead he propped up on his elbows. "I want you to think over the past year, Stephen. Have I been a worse friend than before or better?"

Stephen clenched and unclenched his fists at his sides. "Well, we had more competition before, but you didn't mind if I won. This last year, you kinda switched focus on a few things. I tried to understand when you quit baseball. You've had to help your mom, but you've still made time for us to hang out."

Eric reached up his hand, and Stephen pulled him to his feet.

"Right."

The bench vibrated and Eric retrieved his phone from his bag and answered it. "Hey, Mom. Yes, we're almost done. Sure, I'll walk to the store. Be home soon. Yes, ma'am."

Stephen felt bad. Eric really helped his mother. "Gotta go?"

Eric took off his gloves and stuffed them into his bag. "Yeah."

"If all these collages and stuff aren't about Whimsy, what's this treasure hunt all about?"

Eric's eyes radiated with something Stephen didn't understand. Why wouldn't he tell him?

"Is it about church, Eric? We all go. I've told you before—I'll join sometime, when—"

"When *you're* ready?"

"Oh, I get it now. But *you had*—wait—it's not *that* ready we're talking about, is it?" Stephen rubbed the back of his neck and spit on the ground. "\Man, I just don't get it. Any of it."

Eric adjusted his gym bag on his shoulder. "Later."

Stephen never forgot that day.

The next month, Eric and his mom moved two hours away for her new job.

They still texted on and off and talked once a week, but their friendship changed.

Stephen turned his head at the sound of the back screen door. Whimsy trudged over to him, followed by her faithful dog.

"Mom said to remind you about your haircut."

He swung his legs over the side of the hammock and stood. "I remembered. Just about to leave."

"Tell Mr. Neil to give you a military haircut."

He grimaced. "You know I don't like it too short."

She took his place in the hammock, but instead of lying down; she balanced her petite frame in the middle, and sat with her short legs curled beside her with Paws on her lap. "Just thought you might want to try it."

He turned and made a face at her. "Whatever, Whimsy. Gotta go."

Her voice stopped him.

"Could you drop Julie and me at her grandmother's about six tonight?"

Stephen stopped again and shifted his weight from one foot to the next. He took a deep breath and examined the blue of the sky for a moment before turning back. "Whimsy, I've got a date with Jennifer tonight. I'll be glad when you get your license next year."

His sister nodded. "Me too, but can you drop us tonight?"

"Okay, but you better be ready to go. I pick her up at six-thirty."

He strode toward the house without waiting for her to respond.

As he grabbed his keys and phone off the table, he noticed Whimsy's cell phone beside them. It dinged with a notification. He hit the button. It showed a follow-up message from their mom: *Did you remind him?* The one above it said: *Remind your brother about his haircut appointment.*

He shook his head and tossed her phone back on the table. His mom knew he didn't carry his phone when doing yard work. He learned his lesson when his old one fell out of his pocket and disappeared under the mower. After a quick confirmation text to his mother, he dashed for the car.

Many of his friends went to trendy hair salons, but he still preferred his dad's barber. The shop had three customers in the old-fashioned barber chairs when he entered the shop. Mr. Neil and his son worked on two men he recognized and a new barber named Sherrie worked on a man he didn't know.

"Have a seat, Stephen. I'll be with you in a

minute. Just finishing up on Mike here."

Mike Jones owned a landscape company and plant nursery.

Stephen found a car magazine beside the chair. His dad had warned him about exceeding their data plan, and Mr. Neil didn't offer Wi-Fi, so he tried to stay off his phone whenever he came.

"Hey, Stephen, I wish your friend Eric still lived here."

He glanced up at Mr. Jones. "Why's that?"

The man kept his chin down as Mr. Neil shaved his neck and answered without looking at him. "A friend of mine lives a few blocks from Eric now. He's been using him to mow and edge this summer. It seems your friend is excellent and goes above and beyond."

"What do you mean?"

"Well, Eric couldn't do my friend's yard one week, but asked one of his buddies to do it. The boy did a nice job on the yard, but he failed to blow off the cut grass from the patio, front sidewalk, and driveway. Eric always does this. My friend Sam texted Eric, just as an FYI. In a couple of hours, at dusk, Sam's wife heard the blower outside. When Sam came home from dropping his son off at the movie, he couldn't believe it. He texted Eric again and told him he hadn't expected him to do that. Eric texted back: *It's my responsibility to see the job done right. I appreciate your business*."

Mr. Neil brushed off Mr. Jones neck and removed the cape. "There's not many young men like that anymore."

Mr. Jones nodded and chuckled as he stood.

"True. Come to think of it, there's not many adults with his work ethic anymore." He turned to Stephen. "No offense. Your dad tells me you've done a fine job this summer, but I know he doesn't want you to work elsewhere. I could use some summer help like your friend. My teenage hires haven't worked out too well the last couple of summers."

Stephen stood. "Eric does work hard."

"Sounds like it. Wished he lived closer." Mr. Jones paid Mr. Neil. "Have a good one."

Stephen sat down in Mr. Neil's chair.

"Stephen, I have a car question for you."

Mr. Neil knew how to pick topics to discuss as he cut his customer's hair. The next thirty minutes passed with talk of classic cars and refurbished parts.

"I'll try the wrecking yard to find that part, Stephen." Mr. Neil said, removing his cape.

"Hope they have it. Call me if they do and I can help you put it on your truck."

"I'll do that, my boy."

Stephen paid him. "Thank you, Mr. Neil."

Once in his car, he checked out his new haircut in the rearview mirror. "Jennifer will like what she sees."

~

Whimsy and Julie hurried out of her brother's car. She shut the door just in time. Stephen's tires squealed as he drove away.

"He's so cool, Whimsy," Julie said.

Whimsy quirked an eyebrow. "Cool? Isn't that term a little outdated?"

Her friend shrugged. “I’ve been watching classic T.V. shows with my grandmother during our hospital visits.”

“When does she get to come home?”

“Monday. The doctor says she is well now; it will just take her a bit to get her stamina back. That’s why my mom wanted us to come and do this tonight. Mom’s going by the grocery store tomorrow to bring new groceries.”

“So are we cleaning the house for her tonight? I remember how neat she always keeps things,” Whimsy said.

“Yes, and cleaning out her pantry.”

Julie started for the house and Whimsy followed her to the front door of the red brick house.

“Why do we need to clean out her pantry?”

Her friend pulled a key out of her pocket and unlocked the door. “Grandma hasn’t been home for two weeks, but she also doesn’t check the expiration dates on things.”

“Oh, that’s not safe.”

“Mom says some people use things after the date on pantry items, but she doesn’t want to take any chances.”

Whimsy left her purse in the chair beside the front door and followed her friend to the kitchen.

Julie stopped and sniffed the air.

“It smells a little funny in here. I guess it’s from the house being closed for a bit.”

“I smell it too. Maybe we should open the windows,” Whimsy said.

“Let’s clean out the pantry first.”

Julie opened the pantry door.

"Would you grab a garbage bag from under the sink, Whimsy?"

"Sure."

Thirty minutes later, they had filled a sack from the pantry items and one from refrigerated items.

"Why does she keep so much food and not use it?"

"Since Grandpa died, she has had trouble adjusting to cooking for only one. In addition, she tries to keep extra on hand to have for us or someone else in need. She's just not felt well and has stopped checking dates as she should."

Whimsy hugged her friend. "I'm sorry; I didn't mean to sound judgmental. My mom has been so busy at work; I have caught a few things out of date in our pantry too. But you know what this makes me think about?"

"No."

"My devotional about when God sent manna. You know the story?"

"Uh huh, kind of."

"The manna fell to feed the people but they could only eat it that day. Any left went bad."

"Oh, yeah, except on the weekends, when it remained good for two days."

Whimsy giggled and bumped her friend with her shoulder. "Kinda."

Julie laughed.

"He provides all we need. Sometimes we don't trust and keep things in our lives and pantries longer than necessary because of fear and self-reliance. His provisions are always on time and perfect in abundance," Whimsy said.

Julie's eyes sparkled. "Just like the loaves and fishes, too. Baskets left over."

"Right." Whimsy loved how Julie always got what she said. They started finishing each other's sentences during youth group four years ago. Julie's family had moved to town to be close to her grandparents due to Julie's grandpa's health. They'd lost him the next year.

Julie finished tying the second sack and handed it to Whimsy. "Let's take these outside."

Whimsy opened the hinged lid on the city provided trash can and hoisted the heavy sack up and in with a thud.

Julie did the same and flipped the lid closed. "Hey, Whimsy—talking about provision, do you think the provisions of the cross; I mean the atonement, covers everything?"

The familiar inner stirring quickened. "Yes, I do, Julie. Don't you?"

"Yes, but I don't think my grandmother does. She keeps talking about how she's failed the Lord in her life, even though she's tried to live a good life. She's afraid she doesn't have enough time to redeem herself from those mistakes."

"Does she know the Lord?"

"I think so. She became a Christian young."

Whimsy sighed. "It's hard to understand why so many don't get it. He did everything needed, and we have to trust in the absolute totality of His blood's covering. We make Him the saddest when we don't have faith."

"So is it okay to do whatever you want?"

"Julie, you know better! There is a difference in

trying to live in the way He taught and stumbling a bit and choosing to live an out and out defiant life. "

Julie looked at her with tears coursing down her face. "Could we pray for her?"

"Absolutely!"

After they prayed, they went inside and started on the dusting and vacuuming. They forgot about opening the windows. Whimsy had finished all the carpeted floors except for the hall leading to the guest bedroom by the door to the garage. A stronger odor reached her during her last pass over the hall carpet. She pushed the foot button on the vacuum, turning off the noisy machine. A few more sniffs led her to the closed door.

"Julie, come here. I think I smell gas."

Her friend padded down the hall and joined her, dust rag still in hand. She sniffed. "You're right. It must be her hot water heater in the garage." Julie reached for the doorknob.

Whimsy stopped her. "No, I think we need to call your mother. If we open the door with a smell that strong, it might not be safe."

Julie's eyes widened. "Maybe we should get our things and go outside to call after we open some windows."

Within twenty minutes, Julie's parents arrived and five minutes later, a man from the gas company pulled up in his truck. Mrs. Parker kept them outside as Mr. Parker and the man checked the house and garage. A few minutes later, the two men came through the front door.

"You girls are lucky. There is a definite leak. We will open the garage from the outside. You were right not to open the connecting door into the house," the man from the gas company said.

Mr. Parker clasped his hands together and looked at Julie. "It looks like we won't be able to bring your grandmother here on Monday. They said it will be at least midweek before they can clear the house for her return."

Mrs. Parker bit her lip. "Tom, what will we do about Monday night? Julie planned to stay with her while we are out of town. We won't be home until lunch time on Tuesday."

"I wish the painters weren't coming to our house on Monday morning. Can you cancel them?" Mr. Parker said.

"No, not with such short notice. The fumes will be too strong for anyone to stay there."

"Let me call my mother. You're like family. I bet they can stay at our house," Whimsy said.

"Isn't your dad coming home this weekend?" Julie asked.

"Yes, but he leaves again on Monday morning."

Julie frowned. "But you only have a twin bed in your guest room. "

Mrs. Parker glanced at her daughter and back Whimsy. "She's used to a double bed at home."

"They can use my room. I just got a new queen bed last month," Whimsy said.

Julie made a face. "I can't sleep with Mamaw. She snores and has to sleep on this wedge pillow." She glanced at her mother.

"Julie Ann!"

Whimsy tried not to laugh. "As long as she is well enough not to need Julie with her during the night, I can sleep with my mother, and Julie can have the guest room. It is just down the hall from my room. Stephen's room is next to mine, so if your grandmother calls for you, he can come get you."

"I hope not." Julie turned red. "Anyway, she seems eager to be home and is feeling well now."

Mr. Parker frowned. "Mother will be frustrated about all of this, but she does love all of you. Do you mind if I call your mother, Whimsy?"

"Not at all."

He walked to the driveway to make the call. Mrs. Parker nodded as they watched him talk on his phone. "He's not biting his lip, so it means things sound good."

Julie grinned as he turned and gave them a thumbs-up as he finished the call.

Mrs. Parker picked up her purse off the porch settee. "Okay, girls. You've worked hard. We are taking you for pizza before dropping off Whimsy. Mr. Hunt, the gasman, will be here for a bit and will lock up when he's finished."

~

The Parkers dropped off Julie and her grandmother on Monday morning. Lila Parker held her son's arm as she entered their house. Her short gray hair curled in various directions, so unlike her usual neat teased and set style. Whimsy had visited her house many times during the past four years, and she liked the studious and talkative lady. The elder Mrs. Parker had also been to their home many times before with Julie and her parents.

"Hello, Lila, my husband had to leave on a business trip this morning, but sends you his best.

We are so happy to have you with us," Whimsy's mother said.

"I hate putting you out like this, Robin," Mrs. Parker said. She stepped away from her hovering son.

"You haven't. I arranged to go to work after lunch."

Whimsy loved the way her mother always put others at ease and wanted to do the same. She stepped forward. "My room is all ready for you, Mrs. Parker."

Mrs. Parker smiled at her. "I am grateful for your hospitality." She shook her head at the arm Whimsy offered. "Thank you, but I can make it on my own. Just walk with me, dear. I do hate putting you out of your room, though."

Whimsy walked with her toward the hall. Julie followed them, carrying her grandmother's wedge pillow.

"It's a privilege to have you. We have breakfast ready for you. I'll bring your tray once we get you all tucked into bed," Whimsy said.

"That is unnecessary, but so nice. My appetite is returning. I didn't realize how much this had taken out of me until leaving the hospital today. I'll get my stamina back in a few days. I've got to. You know I've almost finished our family's genealogy. Tom brought my notebooks. I haven't been able to work on it during my hospital stay."

Julie cleared her throat, and Whimsy glanced back to see her roll her eyes. Her grandmother's obsession with their family's history embarrassed Julie. Whimsy found it charming and interesting to a degree.

Whimsy stopped at her doorway. “Here we are. I have a new bed.” She stepped to the side so the sweet lady could precede them into the room.

Julie placed her grandmother’s pillow on the bed as the older lady sat on the soft comforter and bounced a few times.

“Very nice, Whimsy. Julie said your old one squeaked.”

Julie’s mother scurried in and set down her mother-in-law’s overnight kit and suitcase plus a large tote bag. A smile came to Whimsy’s face. The bag resembled her art bag.

“Mother Parker, I’ll help you get on your gown, but Tom and I have to hurry,” Julie’s mother said.

“Thank you, Sylvia, but I can do it. I am tired of all the fussing over me.” Mother Parker grinned at Whimsy and Julie. “But I’ll let the girls pamper me a bit though.”

“I’ll help Whimsy with your breakfast tray, Mamaw. We’ll be right back,” Julie said.

“Thank you, girls.”

Julie trailed her to the kitchen where Mr. Parker stood going over Mamaw’s regular medicines with Whimsy’s mother.

Her mother motioned them over. “You and Sylvia get on the road, Tom. I’ll go over these with the girls as they will be with her today. But if I know your mother, she will want to get them for herself.”

“You’re right. Thanks again, Robin.” He turned to Julie and kissed her forehead. “We will see you tomorrow. Love you.”

"Be careful, Dad."

Whimsy's mother reviewed the list and coded pillbox with the girls before they fixed Mrs. Parker's tray. Stephen stumbled in wearing a wrinkled t-shirt over his pajama pants.

"Stephen, we have guests."

"I put on a shirt, Mom." He yawned and grinned when Julie turned red.

Whimsy made a face at him before following Julie to take the tray to Mrs. Parker.

The sweet woman sat in the middle of the bed propped against her wedge and Whimsy's pillows. Julie sat on the side and turned to place the tray across her Mamaw's lap.

"I am sorry you must stretch, my dear. Your mother thinks I will fall off and would not let me sleep on my favorite side of the bed."

"Which side is that, Mrs. Parker?" Whimsy asked.

"The right," Mrs. Parker said. She winked at her. "I'll move over once the coast is clear."

Whimsy assessed her newly rearranged room. Half of the blue wall now accented the headboard, with the blue door of her small closet to the left of the headboard when facing the bed. When lying on the bed, the yellow wall stood to the left, the purple wall a few feet from the footboard, and the red wall framed the doorway on the right side of the room. They'd moved her vanity from the left side of the red wall to join the dresser against the purple wall. Thanks to her new larger bed, only a small space remained between the left side of the bed and the yellow wall. Each wall still held the same significance, but the vantage point from the bed changed with the repositioning of the furniture.

"Well, if you turn on your right side—even while staying in the middle of the bed—I hope you like red."

"I try to stay on my back when lying on my wedge to help my reflux, but I do roll on my side sometimes. Your red wall *is* to my liking, young lady. In my younger days, I often wore red."

A familiar tingle and burst of joy engulfed Whimsy for a moment. "Wonderful!"

"I do have one question though, dear." Mrs. Parker inclined her head. "Why are there four nails on the red wall without anything on them?"

Whimsy shared a smile with Julie. "Originally, my mother had nursery pictures grouped on the wall. When we took them off, I stopped her from removing the nails."

"Why?"

"Their position reminded me of the nails in the cross."

Mrs. Parker tilted her head, appraising the wall. "I see it."

Julie removed the napkin from the tray and handed her grandmother a fork. "You need to eat, Mamaw."

"Yes, sweet girl. Will you please bless this food?"

Julie gave her a fond smile, and they bowed their heads and said the blessing.

"Whimsy—"

They lifted their heads to find Whimsy's mother in the doorway.

"I'm sorry."

"It's fine, Robin. We blessed this fine breakfast. Thank you for it," Mrs. Parker said.

"My pleasure. Do you need anything else?" Mom said.

"No, dear. Julie will make sure I eat enough."

"Good. Then if you don't mind, I am going to head off to work a bit sooner than expected. They called and need me now. Whimsy, let me show you where I put lunch in the fridge."

Whimsy followed her mother to the kitchen. Stephen sat at the table shoveling eggs and toast into his mouth.

"I sure wish we had this every morning," he mumbled while chewing.

"Don't talk with food in your mouth." Their mother frowned at him before opening the fridge to show the casserole to Whimsy.

Stephen finished and stood, stretching and popping his back. He headed back to his room, leaving his plate and glass on the table.

After seeing her mother off, Whimsy returned to the kitchen and sighed. There were too many dirty dishes and pans for the dishwasher. She'd just hand wash them like they did at her Grandma M's house.

Julie found her with her hands deep in the warm soapy water ten minutes later.

Her friend set the breakfast tray on the table and grabbed a kitchen towel. "Mamaw and I like to wash and dry sometimes too."

"How is she?"

"I think she'll sleep. She just tires more easily right now. But she can be home by herself once the gas problem is fixed. The doctor told Dad her stamina should return soon. Her blood count has been down, and she has some mild heart issues. They think they have things stabilized. I pray they do."

Whimsy rinsed the soap off a plate and handed it to her. "I've been praying too."

Julie added the dried plate to the stack on the counter. "Thank you."

Stephen entered with wet hair and a small piece of tissue stuck on his chin. The ever-debatable need to shave had started at the beginning of summer. Whimsy's nose caught a crisp, sporty scent and she grinned. Whom did he want to impress? She glanced at her blushing friend. Oh no, he didn't!

"How's Jennifer, Stephen?"

He shot her a warning look. "She's fine."

Julie ducked her head and polished the same glass for a second time.

Stephen grabbed his keys off the table. "Hey, Julie, you wanna go to the store with me. Mom left me her list for the week. Your grandmother is sleeping. I peeked in on her. I'm sure *Whimsy* won't mind."

"I—" Whimsy started, but Julie shot her an imploring look when Stephen glanced down at his phone. "No, I don't mind. As long as you let Julie hold your phone."

Stephen tossed Julie his phone. "You ready?" He made a face at Whimsy as Julie caught the device.

Whimsy shook her head and said a quick prayer. Julie's crush on her brother puzzled her, but she'd be there for her friend, and she'd have to double up on prayers for her brother. She did not know the future, only little bits of knowledge. Her brother had battles coming. She *knew*, but she could not equip him. Whimsy didn't know the details. She bowed her head. When she looked up and out the window over the kitchen sink, a dove flew onto the telephone pole by the backyard fence. She smiled and finished the dishes.

An hour later, Stephen and Julie still had not returned. Mrs. Parker continued to sleep. Whimsy grabbed her phone and texted Stephen. Julie called her.

"We took our time in the store and are on our way. How's Mamaw?"

"She's still sleeping. We will need to give her medicine before lunch," Whimsy said.

"Okay, see you in a bit," Julie said.

Whimsy laid her phone on the table.

"Julie? Whimsy?"

She heard Mrs. Parker calling from her room and hurried down the hall.

"Yes, ma'am."

Mrs. Parker sat on the side of the bed, patting her mushed curls on her head. Her eyes looked behind Whimsy. "Where's Julie?"

"She rode to the grocery store with my brother."

A knowing look emerged on the older woman's face. "Ah, yes. Stephen. She's mentioned him."

Whimsy grimaced. "I bet she has and wish she hadn't. He's not a troublemaker or anything like that. He's just—"

"I also had an older brother." Mrs. Parker

smiled. "Only time will tell my dear. Thank the Lord, my brother turned out just fine. I'm sure yours will too."

Whimsy shifted from foot to foot. "Do you want me to help you to the bathroom? I know I'm not Julie, but when Julie said they'd be here in a bit. I don't know how long that is."

"Well, my dear. I have learned to make do. Besides, I won't fall. I get tired, but the bathroom is right across from your room. I should be fine."

"Are you sure?"

Mrs. Parker stood and reached for Whimsy's arm. "If it will make you feel better, I'll let you walk me there. Let's go."

The rail attached to the outside of the shower door beside the toilet helped assure Whimsy of a grip for Mrs. Parker. Still, she wanted to be certain without embarrassing her.

"Are you sure you're okay on your own?"

"Yes, dear, I appreciate it. You may wait outside now."

They both laughed as Whimsy left. Where were Julie and Stephen?

Whimsy heard the toilet flush and the water running in the sink. The door opened. Rested brown eyes, with a bit of a twinkle in them, met hers as Mrs. Parker opened the door.

"Now, I feel much better and ready for a chat."

Whimsy helped her back to the bed and propped pillows behind her. "What do you want to talk about?"

Mrs. Parker pointed toward the large tote bag. "My genealogy work. Bring my bag and I will show you our Genealogy Pedigree charts so far. I have worked on both sides, so Julie and her father can have both her grandfather's and mine. I'm afraid mine doesn't go back as far as his. You know many records were burned during courthouse fires and due to war."

Whimsy brought the heavy bag and placed it on the bed beside her. The bag toppled and black notebooks toppled onto the mattress. She sat on the foot of the bed and handed them to Mrs. Parker. "Do you go back to any royalty?"

"My genealogy doesn't, but my husband's does," Mrs. Parker said. She opened one of the notebooks. "Here let me show you."

For the next thirty minutes, Mrs. Parker showed her the portions of the charts she'd completed and the proud accomplishments of certain relatives, as well as the few whom the family didn't know much about or wished they didn't know.

"And this is a book I just received." Mrs. Parker dug in her bag and pulled out a thick volume. "The author is related to my late husband, and we are mentioned in it. She went overseas to trace their relatives. We—" She stopped and put her hand to her mouth. "Julie will not be happy with me sharing all of this with you. You may not think genealogy is interesting."

Whimsy patted her hand. "Yes, I do, to a point. You know the Bible lists lots of genealogy in the Old Testament and some in the New Testament, so it is important. But my grandmother drew my attention to something interesting. The key to its importance is really culminated in the listings in the

New Testament."

"What do you mean?"

"Well, in Matthew, it lists Jesus's genealogy from Abraham to Jesus. Then in Luke, after Jesus's baptism, it lists His genealogy again, but lists it in reverse order tracing all the way back to God. Both are through His adoptive father Joseph, who the world first viewed as His father. Now, from what I understand, some people who do genealogies, like to focus on the heirs to royalty in their lines and others each relative. Some people see that in these. I don't know about all that, but what makes me giddy is when you think how God adopts us into the lineage of Abraham through Jesus's blood, making us His children. We share the most important lineage traced all the back to creation and forward to eternity."

The tissue paper hands laid aside the notebook and papers and reached for Whimsy's hands and tears filled Mrs. Parker's eyes. "Oh, my, you *are* as Julie said. And you're right, most of my genealogy friends search for what they call "gateway" ancestors tying them to royalty."

"That's so wonderful! But they're looking for the wrong one," Whimsy said.

"Why, dear?"

"Jesus is our Gate and the Way."

"What a clarifying perspective, sweet one. That brings me to something I want to ask you. My dear, I came to know the Lord as a girl. I know how the blood covers what happens before our conversions. The only thing that pains me is how I have failed Him since then. I've tried, but I've stumbled. You may not know I had married and divorced before I met Julie's grandfather. I have marred her lineage and my walk there. Plus in other ways. Do you still think I'm in the spiritual lineage? Part of the family?"

Whimsy swallowed. "Mrs. Parker, I am not a theologian, but I have a question for you. Have you ever stopped trying to live for Him?"

"No. But I've failed."

"You've read the scriptures. Many fail. What's important is to finish with strong faith, not in yourself but in Him. You must seek the treasure. I do know you are ready."

"I'm not sure what you mean. If we have found Him, we have found the Treasure."

Whimsy stood. "Yes, ma'am, He is everything. Still, there is something He wants us to lay hold of—so to speak—as His children. Many become defeated and miss this treasure. The Enemy wants us defeated and in turmoil. Tornados of dark forces keep eyes within them, viewing only the chaos."

The sound of the key in the front door alerted them to Julie and Stephen's arrival. Julie hurried to them and sat on the bed beside her grandmother.

"I am sorry we took so long," she said.

Whimsy and Mrs. Parker looked at each other and burst out laughing.

"No, you aren't," Whimsy said.

Stephen appeared in her bedroom doorway. "What's so funny?"

Julie ducked her head.

Stephen slumped against the doorframe.

"Hello, young man. Whimsy tells me you're her

brother," Mrs. Parker said.

He straightened under Mrs. Parker's scrutiny. Whimsy smiled and stood.

"Yes, this is my brother Stephen."

Julie also stood. She tucked a strand of hair behind her ear and licked her lips. "This is my grandmother, Stephen."

Whimsy glanced from Julie to her brother. She compressed her lips to block the laughter dancing inside of her.

Stephen bobbed his head and wiped his hand on his jeans before he stepped forward and offered it to Mrs. Parker. "Nice to meet you, ma'am."

"Likewise," Mrs. Parker said as she shook his hand. "Now, if you wouldn't mind bringing my medicine. I believe it is time for it."

Julie looked at her watch. "I am sorry, Mamaw. Dad will not be happy with me."

"Not to worry, Julie. Whimsy has kept me company."

Whimsy grabbed Stephen by the arm. "Julie can stay here with you, Mrs. Parker. We will go get your medicine, and I will put my mother's casserole into the oven to warm for our lunch."

The rest of the day passed without incident. Stephen watered the lawn and talked on the phone, while Julie and Whimsy watched old reruns on the television in the living room. Mrs. Parker napped. Whimsy made dinner and had it ready when her mother arrived home. Julie helped Mrs. Parker get a bath. Afterward, she felt well enough to sit at the table for dinner.

"Whimsy I noticed some interesting collages on

your walls. I meant to ask you about them but once I started telling you about our genealogy—"

"Mamaw, you didn't!"

Whimsy smiled at Mrs. Parker. "It's fine, Julie. I enjoyed it."

Stephen snickered. "Don't worry, Julie. If Whimsy gets started about her collages, your grandmother will be well matched."

"Stop it, Stephen. Whimsy only helps start the collages. Others make them," their mom said.

"Really? Has Julie made one?"

"No," Whimsy said.

Stephen's eyebrows shot up. "Well, well," he said, giving Whimsy a pointed look. "Is she not ready either?"

"We've never even talked about *me* making one. Have we, Whimsy?" Julie flashed her a confident smile.

Whimsy returned her friend's smile and glanced over at her brother. She wished he understood. "Julie doesn't need one now, but if she ever does, she *is* ready." She turned to Mrs. Parker. "If you'd like, I can show you my supplies. I bet you could make a nice one."

Stephen threw down his napkin. "So *she's* ready?"

Whimsy didn't smile at him. Her heart hurt when she looked at him. "Yes, she is."

Mrs. Parker cleared her throat. "Why don't you show me now? Can Julie help us start it?"

"Yes, ma'am, but I don't think you will finish it tonight," Whimsy said.

Mrs. Parker nodded as Julie helped her from her

chair. "No, I don't expect to."

"Stephen, your sister cooked, so you and I will clear the dishes and clean the kitchen," Mom said.

Her brother groaned but started clearing.

They picked a heavy red collage board. Whimsy reached in her bag and retrieved a ruler, fine black marker, calligraphy markers, and two large pieces of lace—one red and one white piece—big enough to cover the notebook-sized collage board.

"Do you have a blank copy of one of those Pedigree charts you have in your bag, Mrs. Parker?"

Surprise and puzzlement showed on both Julie's and her Mamaw's faces.

"Yes, I do. What are you thinking?"

"Well, I think you should glue it on your board," Whimsy said.

"Do you want me to make a collage from our genealogy? I have an extra copy of the one I've started."

"No, not that one."

"The one we talked about from the Bible?"

"No."

Julie looked a little perplexed. "Whimsy, just tell her."

"It's *your* collage. *You* get to decide what goes on it, but the start I see is the genealogy of those failings you are so focused on right now," Whimsy said.

"Like a family curse or something?" Mrs. Parker asked.

"No, ma'am. Let me see if I can make it clearer. You know the old movie where the main character realizes if he had changed one thing, his whole life and the lives of his family and friends would have been different? In essence, his choices, which he viewed as mistakes or missteps, would have changed his and their genealogy for all who came after. In other words, map possible alternate genealogies from the point of each of those failings."

"I think I understand, but why make a collage of it?"

Whimsy shrugged. This point of free will always remained. She discerned other's readiness. They must decide. "You can choose not to, but now you are ready to do this. The last part will lead to finding the treasure we talked about."

"All right," Mrs. Parker said. "Where's the glue?"

Whimsy released her breath. Joy filled her.

Julie retrieved the blank chart. "Mamaw, let me glue it. I don't want it on your hands."

Whimsy smiled once they affixed the chart to the board. "We better let it dry tonight. You can write on it in the morning."

"That sounds good, and if Tom and Sylvia get here before I'm done, I'll just take it home to finish," Mrs. Parker said.

"That's wonderful. Only *you'll* know when you're done with it," Whimsy said.

"Julie, I need to brush my teeth."

Whimsy went to her chest and pulled out a gown from the top drawer. "Good night Mrs. Parker."

Mrs. Parker stood. "Come give me a hug."

Whimsy felt tears in her eyes as she hugged the

sweet lady. "I don't mean to be perplexing. You need to rest tonight."

"I am sure. Good night, Whimsy."

"'Night," Julie said as she gave Whimsy a quick hug. "I'll head to the guest room, once I see her settled."

~

Lila Parker lay in the dark after saying her prayers, which felt only ceiling high of late. She thought about everything Whimsy said and wondered how one so young possessed such deep peace and certainty. It went beyond the overconfidence of youth. She thought back to her own conversion as a young girl—the utter peace and joy filling and empowering her to share with others. It did not waver until she felt the defeat every time she made even the smallest misstep. She'd pray about them and ask for forgiveness, but forgiving herself seemed impossible. She had even started writing them in a notebook, keeping a record of each. It appeared Whimsy did not do that. She suspected that girl prayed and let go of things at the end of each day.

How could she have ever gotten to this point of living in a dry well of unworthiness, so far down, she could not look up and see or hear God? She knew Christ's worthiness but felt it could no longer apply to her. She had failed Him. How did she start a genealogy of her life from the point of her failures?

Lila's eyes fluttered. She took a weary breath and sleep overcame her. Deep slumber moved her from her position on her wedge to her favorite right side lying position. A while later, a cracking sound disturbed her. She squinted in the darkness. A glow illuminated the red wall.

It shifted like a movie screen and a vision of a parade of pictures from old family albums of both her family, as well as her husband's family flashed across the screen, going back to the farthest points in time she'd tracked, but it didn't stop. It flashed even further back like a rewinding reel.

She noticed key people throughout the cavalcade on their knees and covered by a splash of red. The reel then moved forward in time to the point where she came to know the Lord, but it stopped when she made her first small mistake, the line diverged and the chart appeared on the wall.

A pen wrote this mistake, the choice she made, and traced how her life course would have changed if her mother had not sat her down and told her she wasn't perfect only forgiven; the alternate course moved her away from God. A scene of her mother praying for her flashed—a splash of red covered her. Next, it moved from her wedding day at the start of college to the day she discovered her first husband's philandering ways, but in this divergent, alternate life course shown on the wall, she stayed with him, but he left a few years later. The path of her life diverged on the wall and an unknown life appeared. On the path shown, she never had children, and so many different people and outcomes appeared.

Then the light shifted and Lila watched her second husband's alternate path, where he never met her. So different. Then the pictures shifted again and reverted back to their first meeting and their life together appeared. But at each juncture of failure, an alternative of the events showed. All the prayers she'd felt only hit the ceiling during her darkest periods, danced on the wall as multi-hued sparks to eternity. The pictures stopped after a flash of the events of the past day at the Michael's house showed.

The chart dimmed and the four unadorned nails she'd noticed on the red wall glowed as points on the shadow of the cross. Blood poured down from each, covering all the listed outcomes on the faded chart. Lila understood. She'd suffered consequences, but His redemption covered the missteps *after*, as well as *before* her salvation. His grace worked in her life for eternal outcomes better than she could ever have planned. She understood the gift of *her* life, and the only heritage important to share rested in Him alone. The blood flowing through her veins was never as important as the blood that covered her stains. Lila slept.

~

Stephen did not sleep well. He heard Mrs. Parker get up a couple of times during the night. The second time he got up and knocked lightly on her door before he opened it. The bedside lamp glowed in the dim room, and she sat in the middle of the bed cutting and gluing on a collage at five in the morning. She smiled at him.

"Good morning, young man."

He rubbed his face. "It still seems like night to me. Are you okay? Do I need to get Julie?"

A momentary expression of contrition flashed

across her face. "Oh, dear. I am sorry to have awoken you." Her smile returned. "But I had to get this done for Whimsy's wall before my son comes to get me this morning."

Stephen scratched his head. "Why? From what I know, most take their collages with them. These two are the only ones finished."

Happiness, no, pure joy lit the older lady's face. "That's why I am putting the final touches on this. Mine didn't need much after my rest last night. It's done. I finished the treasure hunt."

"I'm not awake enough for this," he mumbled.

Mrs. Parker paused and set down her glue bottle. "I pray you soon will be. You need to get ready."

"Mamaw?" Julie's voice interrupted. She ducked her head as she passed Stephen on the way to the bed.

"Good morning, Julie. Come crawl in with me. I'm almost finished here, and you can take me to the bathroom."

Stephen cleared his throat and backed toward the door. "I'm going back to bed now."

Julie smiled at him. "Thanks for checking on her."

"No problem." But deep down he knew something felt off, and it went beyond the people in Whimsy's room.

CHAPTER 4

The Golden Yellow Wall

The years sped by in a whirl of high school activities, puppy love romances, and many more collages. Stephen and Whimsy's paths diverged when he left home for trade school and the gap grew wider once she left for college.

Whimsy lost her voice and her heart's song the summer between graduating with her bachelor's degree and starting on her graduate degree in Art Therapy. Dad died of a heart attack.

Stephen came home. After he finished school out of state, he stayed there and worked as a mechanic at a car dealership. Dissatisfaction characterized her brother's personality whenever Whimsy talked to him, which wasn't often. Even now, in their shared grief, he distanced himself from her. Of course, he'd never understood her. How could he? Goodness, she didn't understand many things at present.

She had started her degree full of excitement and wonder, only to bog down in the psychology and humanistic view of the field. If only she'd been able to go to the Christian university Julie attended, her problems with the liberal professors who challenged and belittled her views might not have been an issue. Her tendency to pray as she walked from class to class decreased during the last year and she felt empty.

The steady stream of tears on her face increased as she remembered Dad's words after graduation just a month ago.

"Whimsy never forget who you are. The Enemy wants just that. You've helped so many at this same point. You're being tested. I've never had to counsel you. You've always been my whimsical girl of wonder. The grownup world is full of disillusionment. But you've never really had illusions because of your faith and convictions. Naïveté about this world is what you are losing. That is part of growing up. There is even a scripture in I Corinthians 13 about growing up. I think it is verse eleven. You have a great purpose and I couldn't be prouder to be your dad."

She ended the year worn down, and her grief—combined with a summer cold, which turned into bronchitis and laryngitis—landed her in bed. Instead of taking care of her mother during this month after her father's funeral, her mother tended to her. Thank goodness, Stephen extended his stay to help Mom.

The door to her room opened. She smiled at her mother who came to sit on the side of her bed.

"Hey, sweet girl, I need to talk to you about something; a couple of things actually."

Mom's green eyes filled with tears as she brushed strands of hair from her face. Whimsy stilled the precious hand and sat up in the bed.

She grabbed her pen and pencil from her bedside table and wrote, "What is it?"

"Well, my darling. You and Stephen are grown. Without your dad, I don't think I can keep up with this house. We need to get it ready to sell it." She looked at each wall in Whimsy's room. "The Lord has spoken to my heart throughout your childhood. I know He's used this room and you for a greater purpose than I can understand. But I've prayed about this. My sister called yesterday, without even knowing my feelings about selling this house, and asked me to come live with her. That's when I knew what to do. When Uncle Jim died five years ago, they had just paid off their house; she is able to have someone take care of the yard and upkeep. I'm not."

Whimsy wrote, "I can move back home."

"No, I won't have that for you or your brother. Your father wouldn't want either of you to return here right now. The post office says I can transfer to a job near Aunt Kathy. Everything is falling in to place. Dad's insurance will cover expenses now and his retirement will cover me when I need it."

She wrote again. "When?"

"That's one of the other things. My new job would start there in September. We only have two months. If the house doesn't sell before I move, and you want to stay in town, Julie's parents said you could stay with them."

She picked up her pencil, but her mother took it. "I know your next question. What about graduate school? I know you're supposed to go straight through, but I can't help you with it right now. Maybe we can look at loans and let you start by the spring."

Stephen pushed open the door. "Of course, there's another option." He entered and handed their mother a pamphlet.

"What's this?"

Whimsy slid it from her mother's hand and looked up at him. She picked up her pencil. "You can't be serious?"

He didn't smile. "Why not, Whimsy? It will pay for your graduate degree and although many people don't know it, the Army has an arts and crafts department and the VA uses art therapy to help veterans."

Their mother snatched the brochure. "Absolutely not, Stephen. I just lost your father."

"Well, I'm going."

"What? You've finished school and have a job. Besides, you're antiwar," Mom said.

"I've got to do something else with my life. It's not working right now. Dad knew. We'd talked about it. He'd asked me to wait until Whimsy finished graduate school. I told him I'd be too old, and he said to wait at least until this summer. He didn't say it, but I think he hoped I'd change my mind. But now that you'll be with Aunt Kathy, I can go. Things are changing in the world, Mom. It's not good and neither am I right now. Maybe the combination of military training and fighting will set me straight if I'm in it."

A scene from a dream Whimsy had about Stephen in high school flashed through her mind.

He'd worn an army uniform and had a military haircut. She hadn't thought about it in years. Her eyes met her brother's and he stepped back.

"Whimsy, what's that light in your eye? I'm still not making any collage."

They laughed until Whimsy grabbed her pencil and wrote. "You should join, Stephen and I do know about the Arts and Crafts program. A lady who works for the Family and Army MWR spoke in one of my college classes. It's a great program. Her dad served in Vietnam and took part in the Army Combat Art Program they had back then. It's not the same now. I need to pray about this for me."

Her brother nodded.

Mom took her hand. "Let's pray now."

Whimsy stretched out a hand toward her brother. He shook his head.

"You two do it."

~

Whimsy napped after praying with her mother. The rumble often reported by those who slept in her room roused her. Her eyes opened, and a scene of men fighting with guns and fire from explosions appeared on the lower half of the yellow wall and on the upper half, flashes of the fires turned to lightning and gold trumpets sounded. She glanced at the visceral battle of men in uniforms, like the ones she watched on the news, engaging the elements and the enemy. The rumble sounded again and her eyes opened wider. Angels joined the battling men. They saved many lives by their swords and lifted some heavenward. She cringed watching the ominous force amid the revealed darkness of the

Enemy, who inflicted torment on the minds of those left alive.

The scene changed to a medical tent and hospitals. Her eyes could see the spiritual battles intensified the mental anguish even more than the physical pain. Paper, pens, paint, and sculptures swirled and formed into a wall-sized collage of all the art mediums she'd studied in school. An angel pulled his sword, and as he extended it to her, it changed into a paintbrush. She took it and closed her eyes.

~

Stephen knocked on his sister's door a week later—no response. He opened the door—no Whimsy.

"Mom, where's—" the question died on his lips as he noticed the new collage on the yellow wall—Whimsy's. The detail of the soldiers sketched beneath a stenciled overlay made him tremble. The clear-stenciled overlay had cutouts of paintbrushes, sketch pencils, and clay potter's wheels. When he lifted the overlay, it showed unarmed embattled soldiers, but when he lowered it, these art utensils went into the hands of the soldiers underneath.

Mom came up behind him. "She signed up this morning. Due to her schooling, beliefs, and interests, they placed her on the Army Chaplain Assistant—wait she said they changed it to Religious Affairs Specialist—trajectory for now."

Regret seized him. "This is my fault. She might see combat."

His mother gave him a wan smile. "It seems that way, but I'm not so sure. Sometimes we are used for a bigger purpose."

"God doesn't use me, Mom."

"That's not true, Stephen. The Bible is full of kings and men God used who did not acknowledge Him. It's better by far to know Him and to serve in His purpose in agreement, but still—"

He met her eyes and swallowed hard. Conflicting emotions churned.

"Keep praying for me, Mom."

"I've never stopped." She hugged him.

A bumping sound in the hall parted them. Whimsy entered, juggling cans of paint and sacks. Stephen took them from her. "What's this?" Paintbrush handles and the edge of a packaged tarp stuck out of one of the bags.

His sister's voice still had a slight hoarseness to it from her illness. "We have to get the house ready to sell; I don't think we can leave my walls this way."

Their mother burst into tears. Whimsy hugged her and cried a bit too. "It's not about the walls."

"I know," her mother said.

"Eric once said something like that to me, but *he* said, "None of it is about Whimsy." It sure seemed like it had to be about her, these walls, and this room. I guess I won't ever make a collage now."

Whimsy crossed to him and stood on tiptoe to kiss his cheek. "One day, when you're ready."

"You mean you've never done one *just for you* before last night?"

"No, it's complicated." She turned and surveyed the room. "I'd like to leave one accent wall and if the new owners change it, that's fine."

Her mother looked around. “Okay, which one? They are all bright.”

Whimsy smiled. “The purple one.”

“Really? That’s the first one I’d paint,” Stephen said.

Their mother only smiled. “That’s the one I’d keep too.”

He waved them away with his hands. “Women! I’m going to pick up some food. I’m tired of all the leftovers.”

“Everyone has been so nice to bring meals, Stephen.”

“I know, but that’s stopping now. This is on me today.”

“Thank you, Son.”

“Wait, Stephen,” Whimsy said. “I have some hinged chests in my car that I picked up at the craft store. There are four. Would you get them for me?”

“What are they for?”

“The collages from the walls. There is one of each color—red, yellow, blue, and purple.”

“Why? You could fit all of these into one. Your friends have kept theirs for the most part.”

“Not all—,” Mom said. “I wrote Whimsy because her friends have come back with collages periodically since she left for college. It’s their way of telling Whimsy all is well and releasing things. It used to puzzle me, but not anymore.” His mother smiled at his sister and glanced back at him. “She told me not to put them on the walls until she came home.”

“How many do you have for each?”

“It’s uneven for the new ones, but I have five

for the blue wall, three for the red, six for the yellow, and one for the purple."

"Why just one new one for the purple? You've only had one other one on the purple wall for as long as I can remember. Whose is the new one?"

"William's."

Stephen looked at his sister. "As in your only high school boyfriend? The one who died in the motorcycle wreck your senior year?"

She nodded. "His mother brought it by. They'd found it on his desk."

His eyes widened and his sister watched him. "So, the purple wall is for those who have died."

Whimsy and Mom shared a smile. It irritated him.

"That's one way to look at it," Whimsy said.

He sat the sacks and paint cans next to the purple wall. "So, if this wall is out, which wall do you want to start with?"

Whimsy crossed to the yellow wall and removed her collage. "This one."

"Great. I'll get your tarp spread over the bed and floor before I leave. I'll bring in the chests when I get back with our food."

~

A few hours later, three of the walls were completed. The first coat at least. All three had a hint of the color underneath. The red wall now looked pink and the yellow and blue walls had pale pastel hues.

Peace settled on Whimsy. "We can do the second coat tomorrow."

"You can sleep in the guest room tonight,

Stephen, and Whimsy can sleep with me to get away from the fumes," Mom said.

Her brother wiped the paint from his hands with a rag. "I don't think the fumes will be too strong for me next door if we keep her door closed." He looked around the room. "It sure feels different in here."

Mom smiled at Stephen and put an arm around Whimsy. "It sure does. Oh. Whimsy, I have something for one of your chests." She left and returned with a collage.

"Whose is this one, Mom?"

Her mother's eyes met hers. "Mine. I stayed in here the night after your father passed."

Stephen scratched his head. "I am so confused. Why would you and Whimsy make collages? Aren't they for people who aren't Christians?"

"No, I used to think that too, back when your sister first started them. The first stirrings of those were for the toddlers she played with, who are allowed to approach without question or decision, but the ones coming *after* your sister came to know the Lord, are very different."

"Why?"

Whimsy sat on the tarp covered bed in the middle of the room. "Stephen, your ears and eyes do not see anything other than through the lens of the world right now. When you come to know the Lord, all that changes. Still, even then, we sometimes lose the sensitivity of our spiritual ears and eyes when other things steal our focus. What's worse—and you're not going to understand this—are the shadows of failings and sins we commit *after* coming to know the Lord. Those may cast a long shadow on our souls, feeling heavier than those before. Just remember, there are battles beyond what you have seen or will see, Stephen. Christians must not forget any of their armor."

"Armor?"

His mother hugged him. "I have a feeling the army will show you what gear you need."

"Sure, but what does one have to do with the other?"

"I'll try to give you an analogy like your father would have. You've signed up for the army, right? Are you a real soldier yet?"

He sat down beside Whimsy, giving her a look she knew well. Her brother did not like long parent stories or lectures. Still, their mother waited for his response. He sighed and Whimsy grinned.

"No, ma'am, only kinda. I have to report for duty and complete basic military training."

Their mother smiled. "Right. And when you finish, will you be prepared for everything you might face on the battle front?"

"Yeah, well kinda," Stephen said. "I'll be better once I've been through my first real battle."

"What will you carry into your first real battle?"

"My gear—my helmet, gun, pack, boots, vest, and things like that."

"Who tells you what to take and where to take it?" Mom asked.

"The army and my commander."

"Would you run in to battle without it?"

"Not on purpose," he said.

"Why?"

"Come on, Mom. That'd be foolish. Even with it, some soldiers don't make it, but it gives them the best chance."

"What else gives them the best chance?"

"Following protocol, orders, watching out for your buddies, and never underestimating the enemy," Stephen said.

"Well done. Now, do soldiers ever make mistakes with any of those?"

"Yes," he said.

"But if they try and fail, is it different than if they choose to disobey?" Mom asked.

"Of course. You'd risk a court martial."

"Do they ever consider circumstances?"

"They'd have to have a trial," Stephen said.

"Who speaks for you?"

"An attorney," he said.

"Would he ever take your place and your penalty? Or walk beside you during the consequences?"

"No, that's ridiculous," he said, rolling his eyes at Whimsy. "You disobeyed; you suffer the shame and consequences alone."

Whimsy looked up at her mother, who nodded at her. She reached for her brother's hand. He pulled away, as he often did. Even though it hurt her feelings for a minute, she had to continue. "Stephen, what you've just stated about the army is true for the Christian, but with a huge difference. Jesus has already taken our place. Still, there is a continual battle you can't see."

"Like that song when we were little. You know the one in Sunday school about being a soldier? It can't be." He laughed. She didn't.

"It is."

"So, these collages—what makes you *ready*?"

She stood. "Oh Stephen, I just hope you get saved. Many have a faith so strong they never need to get ready for this."

"Just what do you call this room?"

"Stephen, it's really not this room. He moves everywhere. I've always viewed my room as a gift; a sanctuary for the weary and a portal to perseverance."

He stood. "I think I'll stick to the army I can see."

CHAPTER 5
The Purple Wall

"Michaels!"

Whimsy jerked to attention, dropping the paintbrush she held out to the patient. The months of Basic Combat Training had made her response automatic.

"Yes, sir, Lieutenant Pruitt, sir."

The soldier in the bed saluted the man entering the hospital room.

"As you were." The officer shook the hand of the injured private, whose shattered leg had a frame around it.

"A word, Miss Michaels."

She followed the lieutenant into the hall.

"Do you know what time it is?"

She glanced at her watch and groaned. "13:30."

"What time were you to report to me downstairs?"

"13:15."

"I understand you are diligent in your duties, but we have a plane to catch. Chaplain Fair is in the car."

"I'm sorry, sir. I'm ready."

Whimsy had served as Chaplain (Captain) Fair's assistant, Religious Affairs Specialist, since finishing Basic Combat Training plus the extra seven weeks of special training required. Her stateside work with him and the injured soldiers at the hospital had given her tremendous opportunities to learn during the past year. Due to her talents, he'd even allowed her to shadow the art therapist with the patients, as long as she fulfilled all her duties with him each day. Chaplain Fair seemed to appreciate her attention to detail and her diligence to her duties, so there had been no problems, until her tardiness today.

She climbed in the back seat of the waiting car.

Chaplain Fair raised an eyebrow and looked at his watch. The Army did not like excuses.

"I'm sorry sir. It won't happen again," she said.

"See that it doesn't. We are heading to Afghanistan."

"Yes, sir."

After Whimsy fastened the seatbelt, the chaplain passed her a folded piece of paper and an envelope. "Corporal Hall asked me to give this to you."

A tinge of regret twitched inside of her. She hated not meeting her brother's friend in person before leaving. "So he's awake now? He stayed groggy after he arrived yesterday."

"Yes, he hated not talking to you today, but he scribbled you that note and asked me to give you your brother's letter. Go ahead and read those now. Once we get on the plane, I need your focus."

Whimsy unfolded the note and squinted to make out the less than stellar penmanship of her brother's friend.

Whimsy,

Sorry I stayed so out of it when we met yesterday. Stephen's told me so much about you. It's important for you to know that your brother saved my life this week. You don't need the details. Where you're headed will show you without words. I am thankful to get the chance to come home and see my wife and son again. Keep your eyes and ears alert and your head and butt down. I'm praying for both of you.

Corporal Vance Hall

P.S. Enjoy the picture he sent. You can see me in better shape in it.

Whimsy's heart calmed. Stephen had a Christian buddy. She wanted to tear open the envelope but took a breath and slid her finger under the seal. Tears came to her eyes from the moment she slid the photograph and folded letter from the envelope. She put the back of her hand to her mouth to still her trembling lips. The photograph showed Corporal Hall standing beside the Chaplain and his assistant, the ones Whimsy and Chaplain Fair were replacing. The trio stood inside a plastic lined dirt hole with water in it, more like a trench than a pool. Other soldiers stood in the background. A fourth man sat with water dripping off his smiling face. Whimsy flipped over the picture. On the back, Stephen had written "My baptism" and the date two weeks earlier. She couldn't stop the tears. Chaplain Fair cleared his throat and handed her a tissue.

"Corporal Hall shared your brother's news with me this morning. Of course, you know I would have just sprinkled him."

She took the tissue and smiled. The diversity in the backgrounds of the Chaplains took Whimsy a bit to adjust to, while not always agreeing with the differences. Her opinion did not matter in the Army, only her duty to those over her. So, she kept the differences as a constant on her prayer list and honored those she served with. She pulled out her brother's letter.

Whimsy,

Hey! Boy I bet you are surprised. (Smile) Sis, this past year has been some of what I expected but more what I didn't expect. It's changed me. I tried to drop you a few lines before, but I've never been much for letters. Still prefer texting. LOL. So, I figured you still talked to Mom, being stateside, and I've been able to talk to her some. But you deserved this letter. Let me say, I never saw Tater, I mean Vance—Corporal Hall—coming. He's not preachy. He's solid and has a faith that you see and it doesn't waver. I don't mean yours and mom's does. It doesn't, but it hit me different seeing it in the middle of all of this.

You never could understand how I could know about and not seek salvation. I've never told you that I almost did after you got saved and again after Eric did. Do you know what stopped me? It seemed to me that every other time we were in church, either at our church or at another with family, the pastors kept having those saved as kids or youth to question their salvation experiences. That stopped me. I figured if salvation might not 'take' for those doing it before they're grown, I'd just wait until I could be old enough to decide and remember it well enough to stare them down. My head sure thought about it, and I kept my heart out of it. I've met a few who just made early decisions because they just thought that's what others were doing and those could be in question, but Whimsy, one's like you, Julie, Eric, and Vance did 'take' the first time. They were personal decisions between God and each of you. The Holy Spirit convicted and you responded. Your hearts and heads were ready. There's still a bunch I don't understand, but I have faith now and the Lord is with me.

Love you, Sis!

Stephen

The car stopped. Chaplain Fair looked at her. "Ready?"

"That's affirmative, sir."

She grabbed her gear from the trunk.

~

Rocket fire greeted their landing in Afghanistan, so different from when they left Germany a few hours ago. They disembarked in run and dodge mode. Whimsy's diminutive stature and agility served her well. Boot Camp had built her strength and it had only increased with continued daily work. Part of her job involved the security of Chaplin Fair. It would be wrong to call her just his guard. The scope of her duties exceeded the title. The other soldiers surrounding them really fit the protecting role better. Still, active duty made them part of a unit. It sank in— she now had to watch out for them to a degree, as well as her chaplain. She felt sure Chaplain Fair flinched when they first met, but combative patient situations within the hospital had proven her ability to mediate and intervene well. Still, this first active combat duty experience spurred her adrenaline. She said a prayer and stayed on point in front of the chaplain until they reached cover. The noise level bothered her more than the new smells in the air and the intensity of the soldiers meeting them off the tarmac. She exchanged hand signals with the sergeant as her gaze went to the waiting helicopter. They advanced, boarded, and took off before Whimsy had time to ponder any of it. She acted and reacted within the situation as trained, the chaplain's and other soldier's safety first in her thoughts before her own.

The jarring and noise of the liftoff kept her quiet. She gripped the weapon issued to her on the tarmac and glanced at the four soldiers with them. None smiled, until they landed. Then one removed his helmet, revealing military-cut red hair, and grinned at her.

"So you're Wrench's sister? You handled your first taste well."

Whimsy noticed the soldier's stripes.

"Excuse me, sir?"

"Whimsy, right?"

"Yes, sir."

Her chaplain crossed his arms and addressed the sergeant, "Yes, this is our newest NCOIC, Private Martha Michaels."

The whirring of the departing helicopter prevented a response. She just motioned and went toward the tent ahead with both men by her sides.

The flap lifted. Stephen stood there in a tan T-shirt and fatigue pants, dog tags hanging around his neck.

The sergeant held up one finger toward him. "Wait, Private Michaels. This could get confusing. You can't be on patrol together. Anyway, you have permission to greet your sister, as a brother should before gearing up; you're heading out with my team. Take ten minutes while I get Chaplain Fair checked-in."

Whimsy ignored Stephen and stayed with the chaplain as they walked inside. Another officer walked up to them. The sergeant leaned forward and whispered in his ear.

"Private Michaels, I am Lieutenant Martin. You're cleared to talk to your brother. The chaplain is with me until you get back. We need to get both of you over to the hospital tent."

"Yes, sir."

She ducked back out where Stephen stood grinning, both hands crossed over his chest with his hands tucked in his armpits. He waited until she smiled and then scooped her up in a big hug, lifting her off her feet. She gasped. Her heart filled and she clung to him. Some of the other soldiers lost their serious expressions. He set her down and pointed to her.

"This is my sister."

"What name should we give her?"

"She's already got a nickname."

She smiled at them. "When we're off duty, call me Whimsy."

A short stocky private nodded, "Whims, it is."

"No, Whi*msy*—Whims is fine."

"She's all right, Wrench." The private waved at them. "Gotta get my gear. See ya in a bit."

She raised an eyebrow. "Wrench? You've been fixing things as usual."

He scratched the back of his neck with one hand. "Yeah." A slight awkwardness, almost like meeting someone you'd known forever for the first time passed between them. "Whimsy—"

She wiped away a tear of joy coursing down her cheek. "I know, Stephen." She met his moist gaze and stepped forward for another hug. Shared peace encapsulated them for a moment before his stocky buddy returned and handed her brother his gear.

"Time for work."

Stephen stepped back, placed his helmet, and took the rest of his gear.

"Put on all of it, Brother."

His friend gave her a funny look. "Why wouldn't he?"

Stephen met Whimsy's gaze above his friend's head. "I won't skip a step, Sis."

She nodded and stepped back. "See ya."

His friend slapped him on the shoulder and Stephen lifted his hand and ran for the waiting Humvee.

~

The next three months brought them closer. They never patrolled together, but Stephen heard nothing but admiration for his sister, regardless of the diverse belief systems present. She took care of the unit- from supplies to prayers. The chaplain valued and respected her. Chaplain Fair said he needed her on patrol with him. She handled the dying and wounded well and made quick and efficient decisions in the midst of engagements.

Stephen no longer viewed her as the odd little sister who made collages. Her purpose and calling became clear to him. She helped his fellow soldiers keep fighting, just as she'd helped weary Christian soldiers back home persevere. *Why* each fought, *who* fought *beside them*, *who* they fought *for* back home, and *the truth* beyond their biggest fears made the difference. There had to be something more valuable than the very battles each fought. Why endure the body count and horror of war?

Stephen now understood that, for the American soldier, it involved the need to assure the continued freedom and safety of every citizen. For the Christian, it meant bringing others to Christ, even while they surrendered to the absolute grace and mercy under Jesus's blood each day anew.

He looked for Whimsy when he missed her in the mess line, and found her in the aid station tent. She sat beside Shawn Franklin, a former surfer from California. The guys loved him due to the smiles his rather cosmic views brought. He had a great heart though, and a wonderful way with his service dog, who'd also suffered injuries in the IED explosion. Shawn and his dog had been the least injured, but they'd lost two of his buddies.

They expected the chopper taking Shawn and his dog to the airstrip any minute.

Shawn stopped talking as Stephen entered the tent.

Stephen grinned and pulled two chairs together. He flopped down on one and propped his feet on the other. Shawn remained the sole patient in the tent right now; it filled Stephen with gratitude and trepidation at the same time. He removed his hat and put it over his eyes.

"I'm beat and decided on a few winks in here. You two continue."

Shawn's affable voice resumed. "Yeah, like, I've always wondered about how everyone can fit in heaven now and in the future one you talk about. What if it's something *deep* like, *every* man folds back into Adam and *every* woman folds back into Eve at the end? Like, *every* man and woman since creation is a part of *them*, and at the end, it goes back to *them and God* again. You know, cause they messed up, but *this Jesus* is the coolest dude and took care of saving 'em like you said, so that could happen. Then there's room for them."

Stephen wanted to sit up and see his sister's face but forced himself to wait for her response instead. He marveled at the seriousness of her reply.

"Well, Shawn, you've really pondered this, and in a way, we are all part of Adam and Eve. But we aren't pieces of a new composition of them. Do you have any brothers or sisters?'

"Yeah, one of each."

"Does your mother love them the same?"

"My mom is cool. She's worked two jobs and has made sure we had what we needed after my dad left. I guess she loves us the same, but there are times we make *liking* us hard."

"What I mean is—if she had to choose to never see one of you ever again—would she want that?"

"No, she's worked hard to keep us together. We

did have to go to foster care for a few months, but she got us back."

"Well, if you go back and read, even Adam and Eve's children had problems. One brother killed the other and God remained right there. He didn't stop caring with Adam and Eve. Each child has purpose and are cherished gifts. He wants to bring us *all* home through His Son. People reject and abandon God, not the other way around. As far as the dimension and parameters of eternity, those are in His measurements, not ours, and are certain to be more than adequate."

"Cool. You know my sister got Jesus last year at some crusade or something. What you say makes me want to get to know Him, too. Yeah, I think I might want that and the other stuff you told me about earlier."

Stephen held his breath as they prayed.

He heard Whimsy finish. Shawn continued on his own.

"Amen. Well, all right," Shawn said.

Stephen could hear the excitement in the young soldier's voice.

"Hey, do you think they'd let me video chat my sister before I go? Do you think I have time? I guess I'll have to get baptized later, or at least, let Chaplain Fair sprinkle me before we lift off."

"I don't hear the chopper yet, let me duck out and see if I can bring one of the secure laptops in here. I'll be right back," Whimsy said.

"Yes, ma'am."

A few minutes later he heard Whimsy re-enter, breathing hard. "Here you go, Shawn. Make it quick. Chopper's due any time."

"Affirmative, ma'am."

After another few moments, Stephen heard a female voice on the computer. "Shawn? What happened to you? Are you going to be all right?"

"Whoa, slow down, Sis. I'm going to be fine. In fact, I'm coming home."

Stephen heard a squeal of delight.

"Yeah. Chill, a moment. I've got something to tell ya before we catch our ride"

Stephen startled when Whimsy shook his shoulder. "Let's walk outside."

He sat up, wiping away particles of sand off his mouth before he stood and followed her. Shawn continued talking to his sister and gave him a thumbs-up as they passed his cot. He glimpsed a young woman with blonde hair on the screen as they passed.

Whimsy pulled out a piece of paper from her pocket and handed it to him. A slight tension crackled and he gave her a wary look before unfolding the page. He read and started frowning.

"Aw, man, you must be kidding me. Why now?"

"Chaplain Fair and I are returning stateside . . . because . . . because you are here. They don't want a brother and sister in the same place, it seems your unit wasn't supposed to be here when we arrived. Circumstances and orders changed. Now we have to go. Our replacements arrive today. We head to Germany with Shawn and his dog."

The soldier side of him understood, but the brother side knew he'd miss her. Their relationship had grown. He turned and walked a few feet away and stared at the sand.

"You're ready," Whimsy said.

His mouth went dry and his heart jumped as he turned. "What?"

The sound of the chopper landing made her response seem mouthed. He strode across the few feet between them and jerked his baby sister to his chest, bending his head down, so she could hear him. "Don't say that to me now. What's coming?"

She turned her head and tilted back to look up at him with tear-filled green eyes. "I don't know, but He does. Find the treasure. Come home."

Over her head, he could see Chaplain Fair striding toward them. He released her. She stepped back and mouthed, "I love you, Brother."

His mouth moved, but he knew she couldn't hear him, still she smiled, and he knew that she knew her big brother loved her too. Then she turned and dashed back into the tent with the chaplain to grab her gear.

Within fifteen minutes, in which Shawn implored Chaplain Fair to sprinkle him, they were loaded and gone.

~

Whimsy could see the airfield in the distance and smiled across at Chaplain Fair. She leaned over to check on Shawn. His dog lay beside him.

"We're almost there," she shouted.

He gave her a thumbs up and a smile. She reciprocated before she straightened and adjusted her helmet. As she leaned her head back, a silent prayer lifted her heart.

The helicopter shimmied and pitched. Whimsy opened her eyes as everything exploded like the scene on her wall. Someone took her hand.

~

Stephen glanced out the window of the Humvee as they returned to base camp. The major stood waiting. Their radio emitted a crackle, and Private Manning answered, confirming their arrival.

"That's affirmative. He's here." Manny turned his head to look back at him. "The major wants to see you, Wrench."

The vehicle stopped and Stephen stepped out with trepidation tingling along his spine. His C.O. and the major met him before he took ten steps.

"Private Michaels, I'm here to take you home."

He came to attention and saluted, not understanding but ready to follow orders.

"At ease, Michaels," Lieutenant Martin said and turned to the major. "With your permission, Major."

The major gave him a nod. "See he's on the chopper in fifteen."

"Yes, sir." The officers saluted and the major strode away, leaving them to talk alone.

Stephen's stomach felt queasy. They'd been in a hot zone the last couple of hours. He'd left right after Whimsy took off, but he didn't recall blundering, and he'd followed all orders.

"Wrench, look at me." His lieutenant's voice held—*who*?

Stephen's eyes darted to the waiting chopper and back to the lieutenant's face in slow motion. *Whimsy.*

He couldn't stop the tears any more than he

could slow his racing heart.

"Is she?"

He received a single nod.

Stephen's mind raced. She had to leave because of *him. No!* Bile rose in his throat.

"A rocket took out the chopper. Complete explosion," Lieutenant Martin said.

All he could see right now were flashes of his sister's life with him in the background. No. This couldn't be happening. He could feel his lieutenant's eyes on him and lifted his head, pushing his emotions behind the partition of the soldier side of his heart. A lot remained stuffed behind that partition already. Only God knew what would happen if he ever let it break.

"Thank you for telling me, Sir. May I go now?" he said.

The lieutenant dismissed him.

He couldn't breathe as he stuffed things into his duffel and took one last look around his tent. The crashing wave of emotions ebbed away, and he walked out of his quarters on a beach of numbness. The others returning from the patrol met him. Manny slapped his shoulder. They were family too. They'd all lost her. These guys looked at Whimsy as family just as much as they did Shawn and his dog. He nodded at them.

The chopper and the major waited. He ran toward them.

~

Stephen prayed on and off all the way to Germany. *This is just a mistake.* Once they landed, he half expected to see his sister waiting for him.

Instead, the empty tarmac felt as barren as his heart. His phone conversation with his mother felt surreal. Listening to her cry without being able to hug her almost undid him. The swirl of procedures, protocols, and orders kept him on track for the days leading up to his flight stateside. Information about the debris from the chopper and the remains they recovered did not reach him before he climbed on the plane home.

Corporal Vance Hall met his plane. Stephen had not seen Vance since he'd help carry him to safety. The altered posture and change of cadence in his friends gait confirmed what his friend had failed to write.

"So they took your leg, Tater?" he asked, shifting his heavy duffel strap on his shoulder.

"Nah, that's just an illusion. I'm still in uniform," his friend said.

"You dumb lug. Why didn't you take the discharge?"

"Because my mind is a *terrible thing to waste, and* it seems *Uncle Sam still wants* me, just not in the combat zone. I'm great at IT and Intel."

"I'll just bet you are. Personally, I think you've grown up with commercial propaganda and an inflated ego."

"Could be, but as my relatives would say, 'I's still here, sir' and that's enough," Vance grinned, showing bright teeth contrasted with his dark face, which quickly sobered as his tone grew serious. "We're still here, brother."

Stephen felt a lump form in his throat as their banter turned to his new reality. He glanced at the milling people around them—the noise and movements of normalcy—all making their way in lives still going forward. His eyes met his friend's.

"But *she's* not, *Shawn's* not, *Chaplain Fair's*—"

"Hush." Vance shifted forward and whispered in his ear, "They're someplace better. Now, let's get you out of here before I do something dumb like hug you."

Stephen sniffed and swiped at the end of his nose. He nodded, swallowing hard. They returned to base, where Stephen received his leave papers. He'd find out his future with, or possibly without, the army after Whimsy's funeral. They'd decided to bring her home instead of a burial at Arlington. The army granted his and Corporal Vance's request to be part of the detail accompanying Whimsy's casket home. His leave would start after the funeral.

~

The leaves of bright red and gold leaves on the trees shimmered in the November breeze as Stephen watched from the window of the plane. They gave vibrancy to an otherwise drab and cloudy sky as they landed and moved down the runway to disembark. He couldn't imagine anything harder than when he met the military cargo plane, which brought his sister's remains stateside, at Dover AFB—until now. He bowed his head, praying for the strength to do this.

Vance squeezed his arm as he joined him. A few moments later, they lifted their heads. He leaned his head back and took a deep breath. His friend nudged his elbow and inclined his head toward the window.

"Looks like the whole town turned out to welcome Whimsy home, brother."

Stephen turned his head, and the window-framed scene almost felled him. In the foreground, his mother, aunt, Eric, Julie and the members of a military honor guard stood on the tarmac and behind them, separated by the chain linked fence stood a crowd of at least half, if not more, of the town. They held banners welcoming home not only his sister but also him. Emotions within him burned from an unexpected flash of anger, to immense and humbling gratitude. As some of the faces registered, he noted well-recognized ones, as well as ones he did not know, but knew Whimsy would if she were here. They all held American flags. He sensed someone watching him and his eyes tracked back and found his mother's face. His eyes filled and he sniffed hard, but failed to keep the tears in-check.

Vance stood and Stephen glanced back at the rest of the crew moving toward the door. They waited for him. Vance became rigid and Stephen came to attention as a soldier. They placed their hats on their heads and filed into the aisle, past the crew, and down the special steps set up for them. The captain followed. Once they reached the bottom, Stephen saluted Vance and strode toward his mother. He expected her to dissolve, but instead she took his arm and turned toward the plane where the captain stood with a black switchbox, lowering the flag covered-casket to the ground. Vance and the other members of the Honor Guard surrounded it and stood at attention. They saluted and parted as

Stephen and his mother approached. She slumped against him for a moment and he knew her knees had buckled; he bolstered her as they reached the coffin. Her fingers skimmed the edge of the top as if stroking his sister's face. She turned, sobbing against his uniformed chest. His arms encircled her until her shoulders stopped shaking. Vance stepped forward and saluted.

"Mrs. Michaels, on behalf of our nation, allow me to thank you for your sacrifice."

She nodded.

The formalities continued as Stephen stepped back and the guard lifted the coffin. They marched in rapid cadence to load it in the waiting hearse. Eric, Julie, and Aunt Kathy joined Stephen and his mother. Shared grief encapsulated them from the regard of those watching from the other side of the fence. Shared memories of Whimsy connected them as they watched the back door of the hearse close. Then they moved to the waiting car. Motorcycles and police cars waited to lead the procession. They had decided to have the entire service at the graveside. His mother said she'd talked to Whimsy about this possibility after boot camp and that's what his never maudlin sister wished.

Eric shook Stephen's hand and Julie gave him a quick hug before they climbed into the back seat of the car. Stephen helped his mother and aunt inside before circling around to ride in the front seat with the driver. More signs—thanking Whimsy for her service—and flags lined the streets as they drove at a snail's pace through the middle of town. It felt more like a parade than a funeral procession until they reached the highway leading to the cemetery. People stood outside their vehicles, hands on their hearts and flags fluttered, lining both sides of the long stretch of road.

"Well, Whimsy girl, today is about you whether you want it to be or not," Julie said softly from the backseat.

Stephen turned and they all shared sad, knowing smiles.

"She would have been proud of this for anyone but her," Eric said.

Stephen nodded. Oh, how he understood what his friend had said about his sister all those years ago. "You're right, Eric. It's not about her."

"No, it's about Him," Mom said with a smile. True joy sparkled amidst the sorrow in her eyes. "She is with Him and your dad now."

The car slowed and Stephen turned in his seat as they turned into the cemetery. Julie's parents and many of their closest childhood friends stood close to the erected tent-covering over the gravesite. He didn't know several of the others in uniform. Then the car stopped. He seated his mother and aunt, but instead of sitting with them, he stood at attention behind their chairs. What followed seemed too real and surreal at the same time. The double-time cadence of the six Honor Guard members who carried his sister's coffin mirrored his racing heart. Each sidestepped as they transferred it onto the lift platform over the grave, untucked the flag, and held it suspended over the coffin while their minister spoke. The words narrated her life and Stephen once again realized how much he had missed of his sister while living in the same house. But regrets gave way to joy at the minister's final words about Whimsy.

"What remains of the Whimsy Michaels we knew came home today, but her true homecoming came the day her soul left this world. We are truly the ones waiting to go home. She's already there. Let us pray."

Once the prayer ended, the order, "Present arms," rang out. His mother flinched as the gun salute commenced, and Julie passed her a tissue as "Taps" played.

The call to "Order arms" came. The honor guard folded the flag with solemn precision. The last man held it to his chest.

Their minister said, "Please be seated."

The flag passed back to the first member of the guard who saluted and presented it to Corporal Vance Hall, who saluted and turned to Stephen's mom. Vance knelt, one gloved hand on top of the flag and the other on the bottom. He spoke in quiet tones for her alone before passing the flag to her. He then stood, saluted, and pivoted. The Honor Guard filed out in unified cadence. Corporal Hall saluted the soldier who passed him a velvet pouch. He pivoted again and turned back to Stephen and Whimsy's mom.

"These are the shells of the bullets fired today." He took off the glove on his right hand and shook her hand before giving her a quick hug, along with whispered condolences. Vance replaced his glove, stepped back, and saluted one more time before he left them.

Stephen stepped forward to help his mother and aunt stand after they lowered the casket. They each released the dirt and single flowers passed to them. Then they filed out and waited with their minister to shake hands and hug their friends and family. His other relatives present, besides his aunt, had driven straight to the cemetery. Stephen appreciated each of them, but wanted to go —wait—where were they staying? He sighed. He'd have to ask.

The last in line were Julie's parents. Sylvia Parker took his mother's hands.

"Are you ready to go now, Robin? The church is bringing dinner to the house for all of your family. They know you are staying with us."

"We are?" Stephen asked.

Eric bumped him with his shoulder. "No, *you're* not. Your mother and aunt are at Julie's. You're with me."

"You moved back? Is your mother back in town?"

"Yes, I moved back and no my mother didn't. I haven't talked to you since you called me before leaving for Basic."

Weariness settled on Stephen. "That's great. We can catch up tonight. I'm on leave for two weeks." He looked around and found his mother by the graveside. After a few more moments, she moved from the covered area to the headstone on the grave just outside it—Dad's. He could not swallow the lump in his throat. Death had become commonplace in Afghanistan. It hurt, but you pushed forward. Here at home—it felt different. He felt the impact on all those they fought to protect. Stephen moved to stand beside his mother.

They stood in silence; the autumn air caressed their faces like a compassionate friend. The smells of life and death mixed in the fragrance from the dying leaves on the tree limb overhead. He looked up at the mixture of green and gold still clinging to the almost barren branch above to the red, yellow, and brown scattered around them and against the fence a few feet away. A scripture came to his mind.

"There really is one for everything," his mother said.

He blinked as her words mirrored his thought.

She smiled, bent down, and picked up a red leaf. "Solomon knew it, but God's seasons and times aren't the same as ours. I'm not angry. I'm thankful."

What? His brow puckered and he rocked on his heels. "Really, Mom?"

Mom reached up and placed a tentative hand on his face and he realized she hadn't been around him. He'd written her about his salvation, but she didn't know he no longer rebuffed hugs and tenderness. His hand covered hers and he leaned his cheek into the comfort of his mother's palm for a moment with his eyes closed. How often he had thought about her whenever he made it through another battle. She reached up on tiptoe and kissed his cheek. He hugged her and the memory of his last hug with Whimsy collided with the emotions they shared.

"Yes, I'm grateful. Your sister's focus was always toward heaven. She accomplished so much in the realm of the true treasures," Mom said.

Tears choked him and flowed down his face as she spoke these words next to his ear. Stephen squeezed her tighter, overwhelming pride and love for his sister welled up inside of him. He pulled back with a smile. "You bet she did, even to the last minutes before she climbed in that helicopter. She led Shawn to a decision right before they left."

"Shawn? The injured soldier on the transport?"

He nodded as she dabbed his face with a tissue.

"Praise the Lord! Have you called his family?"

He looked down, stunned. No, he hadn't and he had meant to. "No, ma'am. They live in California, but I heard they were flying in for his funeral at Arlington. Both his and Chaplain Fair's services are there today. The two other soldiers were flown to their hometowns."

"Well, son, you must call them, and I want addresses to write them, as well as the other families."

"Yes, ma'am."

"Are you ready, Robin?" Sylvia Martin stood waiting behind them.

His mother squeezed his hand and they made their way to where the driver awaited them. After he helped his mother into the car, he turned to look for Eric. Well, well. He couldn't help but grin at the two people who stood on the other side of the car, parting from a brief kiss. His friend looked up and Julie turned and blushed upon seeing him.

"We're engaged," Julie said.

"Congratulations," Stephen said, meaning it.

Eric helped her into the car, but stopped and looked at him over the top of the car. His fingers strummed the metal a few times and he lifted and lowered his shoulders as he took in and released a deep breath. "We were going to video call you both, but Whimsy died the day after I proposed. We'd hoped she'd be her maid of honor and you my best man."

"You got it," Stephen said without hesitation.

Eric slapped him on the back, and they both got into opposite sides of the car. Stephen in the front again and Eric in the back with the ladies.

By the time they finished dinner and shared Whimsy stories and memories, exhaustion set-in for Stephen. Corporal Hall—Vance—had come by on his way to the airport. He'd see him in two weeks. Eric pulled Stephen away about eight o'clock. He rested his eyes as his friend drove.

"We're here." Eric said, switching off the engine.

Stephen barely opened his eyes as he reached for the door handle to open the door. He stopped halfway out and turned to look back at Eric who still sat behind the wheel. He looked over the dashboard at the house again. "You bought it?"

"Yes, I did. Julie and I are updating some things. I'm trying to get it ready before our May wedding."

"She doesn't live here now, does she?"

Eric pushed his shoulder. "No, of course not. I haven't changed. But I hear you have?"

"Good. Yep." His eyes went back to his childhood home. He knew it had been on the market until about six months ago. The first contract on it had fallen through the year before. He opened the car door and got out. He'd come home. Gratitude filled him. He heard Eric slam his car door and found him waiting with keys in hand.

Stephen grabbed his duffel from the back seat and followed Eric to the front door.

"How much have you changed it?"

"You'll see."

Eric unlocked the front door and stepped back to let Stephen enter first. The walls separating the dining room and kitchen were gone. The open design made it look much larger than he remembered. A single couch and a flat screen television on a brown cabinet sat to the left.

"I sure hope you'll let Julie pick out more furniture."

Eric laughed. "Actually, she's redoing a few older pieces. She's got a talent for it. It's her hobby outside of teaching first graders. Yes, I'm all for her finishing touches on things inside, but I get to do all the outside. I've finished the back and will start on the front in the spring. Let me show you."

Stephen followed Eric through the kitchen and out the new Dutch door. His mouth dropped open. The landscaping looked like a garden magazine or a personification of the garden in one of his sister's favorite English children's stories. Beyond the large uncovered stone patio with a fire pit in the middle, plants he'd never seen, in various stages of autumn shedding, surrounded the flat cedar deck. A maze of hedges lined a path to the middle of the yard, where it intersected a small door within a thicker row of taller hedges.

"It's a good thing this patio is far away from the

plants with this fire pit here. What's on the other side of the hedges?"

"Well, I bought the empty lot behind your original yard. Old man Simpson never would sell it, but his children did. Come see."

He followed Eric down the path and ducked under the low door archway after his friend. On the other side, Stephen felt underwhelmed at first. Barren rose bushes and flowerbeds surrounded two small buildings and in between them, a gazebo with a porch swing in it. Eric took him to the building to the right. A greenhouse. The fragrances and greenery greeting him inside amazed him.

"Wow, my friend. Your degree paid off. Botany, right?"

"With a minor in business. I also started to go further, so I could be a pharmacist, but couldn't see myself stuck in a drug store all day. Do you remember Mike Jones?"

"Yes, he owned the landscaping and nursery here."

"Well, I went to work for him with the agreement that when he retired last year, I'd buy the business."

"How'd you do that?"

"Well, two things. My mother had held my inheritance from my grandparents in trust all these years and my dad actually came through and helped me. He's straightened his life out now, with the Lord's help, and is doing well."

"That's great, Eric. How's your mother?"

"She's good. She went back to school and became a nurse."

"Good for her. And congratulations to you and Julie. She's a special girl. Who knows, if I'd have gotten myself together sooner?"

Eric made a face at him. "Watch it! Besides, *you* didn't get your life together. You wised up and finally let Someone greater take over."

All mirth left him. "You're right on that one. I now understand you and Whimsy better for sure."

"Good. Come on, let's go look at my other building."

"Okay," Stephen said mid-yawn. "And then, I'm ready for some shut eye."

"You got it."

From the outside, it looked like a carpenter's workshop. A tall clock-gear sculpture with two rotating arms and spinning tips stood on a pole between the gazebo and the building. Eric didn't say anything as he opened the door and stood back once more. Stepping through the doorway felt like a punch in the gut. Stephen leaned over, placing his hands on his knees.

Eric put one hand on his back and one on his shoulder. "Breathe, buddy."

Stephen shut his eyes, took a few breaths, and straightened. He opened his eyes and childhood memories crashed inside him.

"Whimsy, stop hiding. Where are you?"

"Mom, she's not in here. Yes, I looked."

"Hey, where have you been? I'm tired of you sneaking around and not getting caught."

"Whimsy, you're strange. I can't believe you're my sister."

"Why are they making those stupid collages?"

"Stephen—Stephen, talk to me," Eric said

His eyes took in the four colored walls and furniture. "This is her room. How? Why? *When?* You couldn't have known."

Eric crossed to the bed and smiled as he sat down and bounced a few times. "Not one squeak. You know when I slept in her room, her first bed disappointed me. But that's a story for another time. Anyway, we did this to honor Whimsy after Julie and I bought the house. Your mother got her old furniture out of storage. We'd planned to surprise Whimsy when she came home. Our plan is to use this for grown-up friends who are having spiritual battles and need a place to get away for a couple of nights."

"How do you know it will work like Whimsy's room?"

"We don't. That's up to the Lord. For some reason, He anointed your sister for a purpose beyond anyone's understanding. Her room, I can't explain it. It's plaster and paint, just like the rest of the house. But spiritual battles happened there. I can't orchestrate anything. Your sister didn't. She just lived in total surrender. That is very rare. We simply felt called to offer a place of peace for others with the inspiration of her room. I know these colors scream, but sometimes when something outside you screams louder than what's in you, you let go. We will just pray, wait, and see."

"You know all I hear, when I stand here?"

"What?"

"Me fussing at her and ridiculing her when we were kids."

Eric frowned. “Didn’t you let that go? How were you with her over there?”

Whimsy’s face the first day she arrived, the smiles she brought to others, all of his moments with her—up to that last hug—brought a smile to his face. “I thought I had let it go. Whimsy and I were so good. Really close. Do you know the last things she told me?”

“What?”

“That I’m *ready* and she loved me.”

Eric stood and walked to the door. “Enough said. Let’s get you to your room. Actually, your old room is a mess, as is the guest room. The only two usable rooms are the master, which is mine, and Whimsy’s old room.”

Stephen turned. “You’re kidding, right?”

His friend laughed and motioned Stephen out before locking the door.

Eric passed him on the way back into the house and picked up his duffel for him. Stephen followed him down the familiar hall.

“The bathroom has been redone but is still here and no, I’m not kidding. Here is where you’re staying,” Eric said.

Stephen flipped on the light, noticing the new bed with a lavender bedspread and lilac flowered shams, a refinished rocking chair in chalk white, and three refinished antique trunks in the same white in front of the still purple wall. The other three remained the eggshell white they had painted them after Dad died.

“What’s in the trunks?”

“Man you’re nosy. I’ll show you tomorrow. No

peeking."

Stephen inclined his head. "I'll consider it."

Eric's expression left no room for argument.

Stephen held his hands up in surrender. "You've got it. Oh, if you hear me in the night. Don't come in here. I don't have 'em as bad as some, but sometimes battle dreams get me."

"How are you dealing with them?"

"Day by day. I pray as soon as they wake me and go from there. Don't want to talk about 'em."

Eric slapped his shoulder and gave him a quick hug before he left, closing the door.

Stephen sank down on the bed and unbuttoned his uniform jacket. He retrieved his uniform bag and hangers from his duffel and fitted his clothes to them before turning to open the door of the small closet. Empty, except for a tote bag in the back corner. He didn't know what he expected. Whimsy's clothes? Spending the night in a house he remembered as home resulted in an odd sensation, not déjà vu, but close. He hung his clothes and shut the door. He grabbed a t-shirt and a pair of running shorts Vance had shoved in his bag on the plane. His friend knew he hadn't even thought about packing street wear. At least he'd remembered his toothbrush. He smiled as he found it in the bottom of his bag, but he'd have to borrow a razor from Eric.

After he finished in the bathroom, he took a quick peek to see the mess in his old room before he returned to his sister's. He grinned as he turned back the pretty comforter. If his buddies could see him now—or Whimsy. *Wait a minute.* He turned around, opened the small closet door again, and grabbed the tote bag. This is Whimsy's. It must have been with her furniture when they brought it from storage. He opened it and laughed aloud. Heavy collage construction paper, scissors, glue, dried up paint, drawing pencils, charcoal, chalk, and erasers. He looked up. "Maybe it is time, Sis."

He'd underplayed his own artistic abilities during their childhood. Everyone thought of it as Whimsy's area. Besides, he didn't want anyone to tell him what to do with the doodles or sketches he did free hand. He did them whenever he got bored or angry as a kid, but often ripped them to pieces.

"Okay, first things first." He pulled out his small Bible from his bag. He let it fall open as he often did when unsure where to start his readings. It fell open to the first chapter of the second book of Timothy. The message of faith and grace continued into the second chapter, so he continued until verses three and four jumped out at him. As a soldier, he understood the words well. He stopped and prayed, "Lord, help me decide what to do. I am a soldier either way. Eternally for you, and if remaining in the military, I'll be a good one. Just let me know what direction to go now that Whimsy is gone—I have the option as the sole surviving sibling for either discharge or work in a noncombat capacity. You know where I need to focus. I don't want to let my buddies down. They're my brothers too. Thank you. In Jesus's name, Amen." He blew air between his lips and reached down for the tote bag.

He propped up two pillows behind his back and retrieved a book from the bedside table on which to lay his paper. He stared at the empty page as he tapped one of the drawing pencils on the edge of the book under it. His sister's face flashed and his pencil went to work on the sketch of her. He knocked away his dog tags, which dangled onto the paper as he leaned over it. In a moment of exasperation, he reached to tuck them behind the neck of his t-shirt, but stopped. He removed them, reached inside for tracing paper and a charcoal stick in the bag. He laid the paper over his tags and made a rubbing of them with the charcoal. After he put them back around his neck and under his shirt, he took the scissors and cut out the rubbings he'd made. He glued them on the upper right hand corner of the collage paper above Whimsy's face; he retrieved his drawing pencil and didn't stop. Smaller faces of Shawn, his dog, Chaplain Fair, and other buddies he'd lost appeared as background to the larger picture of his sister's face.

When he finished, it almost looked like those preliminary drawings cartoonists make of their characters from every angle on the same page. They all make up the same character but are reflections from different perspectives. He guessed friends and family were like that too. He'd invested a part of himself in each. But these faces took those parts with them. He'd never get back those lost parts of himself. Just like when he lost Dad. There'd always be something missing.

But they deposited parts of themselves in you too, Stephen.

He didn't hear the words audibly, but they were more than his thoughts. The burning in his eyes forced him to stop. He rubbed them, and placed his drawing and pencil in the tote bag by the nightstand and clicked off the lamp. Darkness filled the room. The one narrow horizontal window high on the purple wall remained covered by a heavy purple drape, just the way Whimsy liked it. No light entered unless she opened it. He missed her.

Stephen flipped a few times before sleep came. A few hours later, the terrors began. Legs, arms, pieces of flesh, and blood covered the ground. His gun vibrated in his hand. Pings and whirs echoed as bullets found targets and shell casings left a trail. His ears rang. Where's John? His best buddy from boot camp. *No, man, get up.* He dragged his friend by the shirt collar behind the half wall. The medic reached them.

"He's gone, Michaels."

The medic took one of his friend's dog tags and put it in his pouch. His lieutenant motioned him and they moved. Fire burned in his leg, just as in all the other dreams, but this time the dream stopped. He heard a different rumble and opened his eyes.

The purple wall across from the foot of his bed seemed to shift and a bright light poured through the now open window. *It couldn't be morning yet.*

Stephen pushed himself into sitting and held up a hand against the glare. It dimmed as reflections of people appeared on the now beveled wall. Each person stood on broken pieces of rock with their backs to him. Not one turned to look at him. Still he knew them. His sister's friend Cindy who died when they were little, Whimsy's high school boyfriend William, Shawn, Chaplain Fair, all his fellow soldiers he'd drawn on his collage, Dad, and last . . . Whimsy.

The light intensified again and, as it did, the separated pieces on which each stood came together until they all stood on one enormous, solid rock. Each person's face lifted toward the light.

A large hand reached out and removed one of his dog tags from around his neck. The hand pulled back, closed and opened, revealing the crushed pieces. Each soul who stood on the rock took a piece until none remained in the hand.

The empty hand once again reached toward Stephen, closed and then opened. Images of the piggyback rides he gave Cindy and her bringing him a rock from her collection to say thank you flashed across the palm. The scene changed to when Stephen helped William pick out a gift for Whimsy his last Christmas and how instead, William had given him a greater gift. William taught him not to look for the most expensive but the most thoughtful gifts.

The scenes continued to shift. Moments shared with his buddies in Afghanistan appeared.

His fellow soldier's stories of home from different parts of the country—those changed him, especially after he came to know the Lord. He'd also been able to lead a few that way before they took the final exit. Shawn's stories about surfing, pranking his own sister and brother had taught him to laugh more.

Too many things flashed when it came to him and his dad. His dad's stories of his childhood, but most important, the faith and strength he'd wanted to ignore—Oh, if he could just talk to him now.

Then flashes of Whimsy started and the light filled the room. Images of collages she made with people he knew and many he didn't know. Their stories played out before him, and he understood how his sister had been where she needed to be when needed, because *she heard what most ignored.*

The scene changed. Whimsy sat at her old vanity table writing in her diary. The pages enlarged. She wrote the day's events, but the words emboldened were on each page: *Praying for Stephen*. He felt the tears falling.

The scene of his salvation and baptism flashed and Stephen heard a song of rejoicing as he'd never heard. Renewed joy filled him. He could not stop smiling as he listened.

The last scene replayed his final hug with Whimsy before she climbed on the chopper. He watched it this time instead of experiencing it. It made him smile even more. *Those* siblings loved each other.

The scenes stopped, but the palm stayed outstretched. He didn't hesitate; he removed his chain with his remaining dog tag and laid it there. The hand closed and opened. A blood stained cross now hung on his chain. He took it and put it around his neck. The light intensified. He looked up, his eyes toward eternity along with the others. A sweet smell filled the air.

He breathed in the fragrance and slept, grateful for grace.

~

A knock on the door woke Stephen. He startled and sat up, disoriented for a moment, ready to spring into action. Eric stuck his head in the door as Stephen threw back the covers and jumped to attention.

"Whoa, man, you're home," Eric said. He pushed the door open and stepped inside.

Stephen sank back on the bed, his heart racing. He cut his eyes toward his friend.

"You're better than a military wake-up committee. Still, turn on some music or something next time."

"Noted," Eric said and glanced around the room. "How'd you sleep?"

Stephen fell back against the pillows and put a hand behind his head. He looked from the purple wall to his friend.

"I'm not sure I did much, but I did. Does that make sense?"

Eric sat in the rocking chair by the door. "More than you know? The purple wall?"

"Yeah, the only one left. At least, in here."

Eric inclined his head toward the wall now behind the headboard. "That's mine—the one that used to be blue back before the she moved the bed. Where's your collage?"

Stephen rolled over and reached down to retrieve his collage from the tote, his dog tags escaped from under his t-shirt and dangled until he straightened. He handed his collage to Eric.

"Was it real?" He fingered his dog tags. "I'm not supposed to still have these."

Eric looked up from the collage of faces to the

dog tags in Stephen's hands. His eyes hid nothing.

"Yes, within the realm of the eternal visions and dreams, but not in the temporal world sense. Did you find the treasure?"

Stephen smiled. "I sure did. It's all there. We have glimpses here but we often miss them. Did you see what I did?"

Eric shook his head. "No, even without you telling me, I know each is personal. The collages are never the same, but the purple wall is the one we all will end with. I'm surprised. The only ones on it before, as my mother says, 'have gone on before us' so to speak. Are you sick?"

Stephen threw a pillow at him. "No, I think it's because I've lost so many. Don't hang mine."

"I won't, yet. Here let me show you what's in the trunks."

Eric lifted the lid of the first one and Stephen got up and joined him. Stacks of collages filled the space inside. He pulled back at the sweet smell coming from the trunks. A remnant of the base notes of the strong fragrance present in the room last night lingered.

"Do you smell that, Eric?"

Eric sniffed the air and knelt by the trunks. The puzzled look told Stephen the answer.

"Neither the trunks nor the collages have ever had this smell before." Eric took another whiff and smiled. "I like it though."

"I think the Lord does too. Did my mother give these collages to you?"

"Just the ones in the last trunk. Your mother brought the ones in the plastic containers Whimsy had put in storage. No, people have continued to bring their collages by Julie's house, thinking she or her parents would give them to Whimsy. Your sister must have still done it in college because people I've never heard of have sent them. I'll add yours to this trunk," Eric said. He shut the lid and turned. "Oh, by the way, why didn't we ever know about your drawing talent?"

Stephen scratched his head, "Well, I . . . I just . . .," he trailed off, "Is that the doorbell?"

The familiar bell sounded again.

Eric nodded. "I'll be right back."

Stephen reached in his duffel and grabbed a rolled up pair of jeans and a shirt. At least he'd remembered those.

The door cracked open and Eric glanced at the clothes in Stephen's hands. "Get dressed. You have a visitor."

"I haven't showered. Who is it?"

"Brush your teeth," Eric said and shut the door.

Stephen cupped his hands, breathed into them, and coughed. Yep, he'd better brush his teeth. He changed clothes in double time, rushed into the bathroom, and then strode down the hall.

A slender blonde woman sat on the edge of the couch with Eric. She stood as he joined them, and he noticed her height came within inches of his. Her face looked familiar, but he knew they'd never met. Clear blue eyes mesmerized him. He stuck out his hand.

"Hello, I'm Stephen Michaels, and you are?"

"Nikki Franklin, Shawn's sister," She said while shaking his hand. "I'm the middle child. Our older brother is—"

"Shasta," Stephen finished. "Shawn talked about you both."

A flash of memories pulled him back to Afghanistan. Stephen's hand shook when she released it. The vise grip in his chest eased.

Moisture sparkled in her eyes. "He did?"

"Yeah, he had some stories," Stephen said. He wiped the perspiration off his forehead and grinned at her. "They made us laugh."

"I'll bet," Nikki said with a soft smile.

"He kept us laughing when we weren't kicking—" Stephen coughed and glanced at Eric who grimaced. He looked back at Nikki. She smiled and he swallowed hard.

"I apologize, Miss Franklin. I'm sorry I couldn't be at Shawn's service. He was a good soldier," Stephen said.

"Thank you. He talked about you in his few letters and emails. Also, about your sister in that last video chat. That's why I'm here. I tried to make it to her service yesterday, but Shawn's finished too late. My mother and brother are still there, but I have to fly back for work tomorrow. You'd left your mother's cell number as your contact number at the base. I called her this morning and she gave me this address. Anyway, I wanted to thank both you and your mother, since I can't thank Whimsy."

"For what?"

"I wanted my brother to come home. I've never seen him as excited as he was on that last chat. It has devastated us to lose him, but because of your sister, he made the most important decision ever. He had a homecoming, just not the one we'd planned." She looked at her watch. "I better go. My taxi is outside."

"What time does your flight leave?"

"11:00."

Stephen glanced at the clock on the breakfast bar. He couldn't explain it, but he didn't want her to leave. "It's just 8:00. Why don't I drive you and we can visit over breakfast at the airport? Wait." He turned to Eric. "May I borrow your car?"

Eric stood and returned with his car keys before she answered. Stephen took them and twirled the metal key ring a couple of times. Nikki still didn't respond. Her blue eyes seemed to assess him to his very core. He closed his hand around the keys. She smiled. His heart flipped.

"I'd like that. I'll go dismiss the cab," Nikki said.

"I'll take care of it. You two go," Eric said.

She shook her head. "Thank you, but I'll do it. The driver has my bags."

Nikki dashed out the door and Stephen went back to the room to get his wallet. Eric followed him.

"This has Whimsy written all over it," Eric said.

"No, it's got Him written all over it. But she'd definitely approve," Stephen said.

Eric nodded. "Let's go help the young lady with her bags."

Nikki waited in the driveway with her luggage and tote bag. Eric unlocked the trunk and loaded her suitcase. He turned and pointed to the sturdy canvas valise still in front of Nikki's feet.

"Do you want the tote up front with you?"

"Yes, thanks. It's my art bag," Nikki said.

"Your what?" Disbelief gripped Stephen and emotion constricted his chest.

"My art bag. I'm an illustrator for a publisher of children's books," she said.

Eric reached over and slapped him on the shoulder.

Stephen chewed on his dry bottom lip for a moment. He picked up the tote and held it out to her. "Whimsy was an artist."

Nikki took the bag with a bright smile. "Wow!"

"Take your time. Julie will come and get me. We both took today off, so just meet us at the Martin's house," Eric said.

Stephen grinned and opened the door for Nikki. She slid in the car and smiled up at him.

"I want to know more about your sister's art. This is amazing."

"You have no idea, Nikki."

Stephen smiled at her and shut the door. He whistled as he walked around the car. Eric gave him a slight salute and started back toward the house.

Stephen slid in the driver's seat and put on his seatbelt. Nikki's phone buzzed as he started to back out of the driveway.

"I can't believe this!" Nikki said. "Wait. We can't go. My app just notified me of a flight delay. I need to call the airport."

Stephen put his foot on the brake, pulled forward, and shifted into park. Nikki mouthed, "I'm sorry" as she waited for her call to go through. He listened as she gave the airline her name and flight number.

"How long a delay is expected? That long? So I can't fly out until nine tonight? Okay, thank you," Nikki ended the call and turned toward Stephen. "They've had a mechanical issue and can't bump me to another flight until tonight. Is there a mall or someplace you can recommend for me to kill some time?"

Bonfire. The word popped into Stephen's head. What? Then he smiled. He looked at Nikki. "Do you mind waiting here while I go tell Eric what's happening? I have an idea."

Nikki shrugged. "Sure."

Stephen returned within ten minutes. A kindred joy to what he felt last night danced inside of him. Nikki giggled, and he knew he must have a goofy look on his face.

"Let me in on it? What's going on, Stephen?"

Stephen twisted in his seat to face her. *Beautiful.* He looked away and back at her.

"I know you don't know me, but I respected your brother and feel both he and my sister would want you to be part of what I have planned for after dinner tonight. Eric is making all the arrangements and invites by texts and phone calls right now. It's last minute, but I want you to share in this with us. If you will allow me to take you to breakfast, I'll try to explain a bit. I'll understand if you choose to go shopping instead."

Nikki stared at him for the longest minute he could remember. A gentle light lit her eyes. "As long as you get me to the airport on time, I'm in for breakfast and whatever you have planned tonight."

The trust Stephen felt from her hit him hard. He remembered her brother's first combat action. The way he followed orders and covered others, including Stephen. Shawn became his brother that day, as well as Nikki's, just in a different way. Whimsy became Shawn's sister over there too. All were family.

"Okay then." Stephen turned and started the car.

He shared as much as he could about his sister and her amazing room with Nikki over a prolonged breakfast and a slow walk in the city park afterward. The changing autumn leaves blazed with the brightness of life and the smells of home, just as the ending of life can leave a beauty bursting in memories and warmth richer than the start. No wonder Thanksgiving fit so well in this season.

They stopped by Julie's to see his mother, and Nikki decided to stay and visit with her while Stephen went to help Eric with the final preparations for the evening. Just a little past five o'clock people started arriving at now Eric's. His mother, Julie, Mrs. Parker, Aunt Kathy, their preacher's wife, William's mother, the mothers of a couple of Whimsy's friends, and some of Whimsy's friends who still lived locally brought finger foods and desserts. Mr. Parker, their preacher, other friends of theirs brought sticks of wood for the fire pit in the back yard. Everyone milled for the first hour. They ate, reminisced, and caught up on each other's lives. At the end of the reception, Stephen and Eric asked everyone to find a seat for the memorial time. Stephen stood.

"Thank you for coming. Tonight, we honor

Whimsy and all of those the Lord allowed her to touch, but more important," he stopped and looked up, "we honor Him. I'm not about to deliver a sermon, I'll leave that to the preacher here."

Several smiles emerged on the faces turned toward him. He ducked his head. Most had watched him grow up, but many didn't know how different he looked at things now.

"Many of you may not realize how long my sister prayed for me. Most of you know how much I needed it." He looked up. "Thank you, Sis. I always will." He wiped away the tears from the corners of his eyes and looked back at the upturned faces. "I came to know the Lord very far away from home. Now I'm here and my sister isn't. I don't understand, but I don't have to. I *trust*. The Lord showed me something last night. But the point is not just about me or about you. It's about all of us living stinky lives covered in sin. We can't wash with enough soap or apply enough deodorant, or perfume to make us smell good to God. The old burnt offerings turned into smells pleasing to Him. Christ became the most pleasing sacrifice and, because He covers us, the stinky smell of our lives transforms into a sweeter fragrance than you can imagine. Anyway—"

"Amen," the preacher said.

Stephen ducked his head, but looked up as an urgency and boldness urged him to finish. "These trunks you see beside me hold unique collages. Most of the people who made them never held an interest in art. Yet they completed them. It took some just hours and others years to finish them—

either when they found the treasure within their crisis of faith or when their lives here ended. All kept their eyes on Jesus. The lives represented within these simple collages have a pleasing fragrance because of Christ. I want each of you to come by these trunks and take a collage to put on the fire we'll light in this simple fire pit. Within this humble vessel, we make a burnt offering to honor these lives and the Lord. It's a reminder of them and for us." Stephen took a deep breath.

"I've written scriptures on the slips of paper you each found on your seats- Ephesians 5:2 and II Corinthians 2:15. Please go home and read them. Once you get started, you'll want to keep reading. It's—so much more—*when you're ready*." Stephen could almost feel Whimsy's hug. "He'll keep us walking until—He takes our hands and walks us home, just as he did Cindy, William, Shawn, Dad" —he pressed his clenched hand to his trembling lips—"and Whimsy. Until then, we are all part of walking each other home. You know, as a soldier, I'm hypervigilant. We all must be. Guard against and fight the Enemy. Protect, fight alongside, and bring your brothers and sisters home."

Stephen heard weeping and looked down to see his mother hug Nikki.

"Eric, please," Stephen said.

Eric stood and took Stephen's place beside the fire pit. He bent and picked up a piece of wood. "It's an interesting thing about wood ash. It can raise the PH and help neutralize acidic soils. Now, some plants grow best in acidic soils and some don't. In my business, I have to know what kind of soil is best for my plants. God knows where each of us grows best. He often has to balance or neutralize things in each of us. Sometimes we need ashes. So tonight, as we honor all of these, let us burn up the temporary and leave the eternal." He smiled. "Just some thoughts from your local landscaper. Let us pray."

Eric's prayer ended, at seven o'clock, the fire sparked, and burst into flames, consuming each collage placed in a silent procession. The trace of the sweet smell Stephen could not forget dissipated and changed as all the materials burned to ashes. A reverent and rejoicing beauty beyond words remained for all present. The embers glowed long after Stephen took Nikki to the airport.

Stephen went by to talk to his mother after seeing off Nikki's plane, so he returned after Eric had gone to bed. He tried not to wake his friend. A small lamp burned in the living room and one at the bedside in Whimsy's old room. He found a framed picture propped against the lamp. It showed him, Eric with his arm in a cast, and Whimsy laughing after one of his ballgames. He smiled. Peace and comfort surrounded him once he turned out the light. The walls did not change. He stared up at the ceiling in the darkness.

"Lord, please tell Whimsy good night."

Somewhere beyond earthly walls, between the temporal and eternal—that exist within God's design and His perfect time—Stephen's little sister smiled.

THE END

ABOUT THE AUTHOR

Lana Lynne Higginbotham (writes in the fiction genre under the pen name: *Lana* Lynne): Lana is a Speech-Language Pathologist and a writer/author. She is the author of these historical fiction novels under her pen name, Lana Lynne: *Home Always Beckons: A New Sunrise (*First Publication 2009; Revised Edition coming in 2018*); Trails of Change: A New Sunset* (First Publication 2010; Revised Edition coming in 2018); and *Sunbeams at Twilight: A Life's Echo (First* Publication 2012-first printing 2012, second printing 2014, Revised Edition coming in 2018). *A Compass of Stars in Her Eyes (*First Publication 2018*)* is her newest historical fiction romance.
Her first contemporary Christian novella is *Whimsy Michaels and Her Amazing Room (*First publication 2018).
Other writing credits: A creative nonfiction novel, written with a coauthor: *Life Between the Letters: The Chuck and Mary Felder Story (*First Publication 2014*)* by Lana Lynne Higginbotham and Mary K. Felder. Blog writer: a weekly blog post (2012-2014) contributor and served as part of the "Venture Galleries Author Collection" blog team (2013) under her pen name, Lana Lynne.
Lana lives with her husband in East Texas. They are empty nesters and proud grandparents. Learn more by visiting www.lanalynne.com.

Made in the USA
Coppell, TX
18 December 2020